Imagining
Iraq
Stories

By the same author:

Fiction

Sanchez across the Street
Far from My Mother's Home
The Deaths of Don Bernardo
Frida
Sister Teresa
I Am Venus

Scholarly books, literary anthologies, and edited collections

Antología de la literatura española.
> *Vol. I Edad Media,*
> *Vol. II Renacimiento y siglo de oro,*
> *Vol. III Siglos 18 y 19*

Milenio
Women Writers of Early Modern Spain:
> *Sophia's Daughters*

An Anthology of Early Modern Spanish Theater:
> *Play and Playtext*

Teresa de Ávila, Lettered Woman
Women Religious and Epistolary Exchange in the
> *Carmelite Reform*

Collateral Damage: Women Write about War

Imagining Iraq

Stories

Barbara Mujica

Copyright 2021

Paperback ISBN: 978-1-953686-01-5
eBook ISBN: 978-1-953686-02-2
Library of Congress Control Number: 2020949124

Living Springs
Publishers

WWW.LivingSpringsPublishers.com

Cover design: Mariana McCormick
Cover image: Bigstock, reprinted with permission

To Captain Mauro Mujica-Parodi, U.S.M.C.

And to the Men and Women of

The Georgetown University

Student Veterans Association

Thank you for your service, your friendship,

and your stories.

Table of Contents

Prologue

During the four years my son Mauro was on active duty, I never slept. I lay awake at night imagining Iraq. In my head, bombs exploded, bullets flew by, injured soldiers moaned and called for their loved ones. Even after Mauro returned, safe and relatively sound, I continued to suffer from insomnia. I would bolt up in the middle of the night, certain that an IED had just gone off a few centimeters away. It took me a year or so to regain my bearings, and when I did, I spent a long time thinking about how lucky I was. My son was home. Iraq was behind him. As a girl, I had dreamed of visiting Baghdad, the city of flying carpets and magic lamps. Now, all I wanted was to put Iraq out of my mind.

But I couldn't. I kept thinking about crumbling buildings and firebombs, about the parents whose warrior children never came back, about Iraqi mothers crying over lost babies. I'd been fortunate. I was profoundly grateful, and I felt that I needed to give back. My son was on the right track. He had just entered a graduate program. Perhaps, I thought, I could help other veterans ease back into civilian life, particularly those who had suffered injuries or didn't have the support that my family and I were able to provide for Mauro.

I first explored the local hospitals, including Walter Reed National Medical Center, located near my home. The volunteer jobs that were available mostly involved handing out cookies and magazines to wounded veterans. These didn't seem right for me. I decided to look at my own immediate community, namely Georgetown University, where I had taught Spanish literature for decades. I opened the Georgetown website and clicked "veteran." All that came up was an article about a chemistry professor who had served in Vietnam. As for veterans' services, there was nothing except a few lines about certification for the G.I. Bill.

During the following months, I visited one office after the other to speak with administrators about veterans. I met with the president of the university, vice presidents, deans, and program heads. All were supportive and encouraging. In the meantime, the campus veterans themselves were organizing. Under the leadership of two Air Force captains, Erik Brine and Karen

Courington, they formed the Georgetown University Student Veterans Association, and I became faculty adviser. Now, when I went to speak with administrators, I took veterans with me. Articulate and insightful, these young men and women strengthened my arguments by providing firsthand experience. Before long, I was attending countless meetings, helping to devise strategies for improving our Yellow Ribbon program and our medical and housing options. Since there was no administrative apparatus in place for guiding military applicants, the association officers and I spent hours counseling veterans wishing to continue their schooling. Soon it became clear that the job was too complex and time-consuming for volunteers who were fulltime students or faculty, and we began lobbying the administration for a Veterans Office. Those were long, grueling, and satisfying days, during which I got to spend hours and hours with veterans. Best of all, I got to hear their stories.

Mauro hadn't told me much about Iraq. When asked questions, he'd change the subject. In contrast, these veterans were talkative. From time to time, one of them would stop by my office just to chat. I had to get used to rough language—some of them couldn't get through a sentence without saying "fuck"—and   to listen without flinching when one of them described a stupid general whose "head was so far up his asshole that he never saw the light of day." In order to follow their conversations, I had to learn acronyms—for example, that A2C2 means Army Airspace Communications and Control and that RAMPART means Radar Advanced Measurement Program for Analysis of Reentry Techniques. Sometimes vets would show up when I was busy or just leaving for a meeting. No matter. Unless I had a class, if a veteran wanted to chat, I would put aside my work and listen. I had spent too much time imagining Iraq not to take advantage of these opportunities to hear, from the perspective of men and women who had actually been there, what it was like.

Some of the stories were funny and sweet. Others were gruesome. Often I was stunned by the detail these former soldiers provided and the anger or compassion they expressed.

"My son never told me things like that," I exclaimed to one young man.

"Oh, I'd *never* tell this story to my mom," he answered.

After hearing that line over and over again, I began to understand Mauro's reticence. It was not unique. As many vets told me, war stories are just not something you want to share with your mother.

Rather than put an end to my imaginings, the veterans' stories nourished them. They helped me to visualize places and people I had never seen and to grasp situations about which I had never thought: the artisan who can't sell his products because customers are too fearful to venture out to the souk; the sexual tension that can develop between a male interrogator and his female interrogatee; the gratitude of a family whose child is rescued by an American soldier; absurd prejudices held by both American and Iraqi soldiers. Eventually, I started writing down these stories, interweaving them with my own conceptualizations. Strictly speaking, all of these stories are both true and untrue. They are all based on actual events, but they are also products of my own obsessive imaginings.

Mauro is now married with children. He completed his MBA and has a successful career. He never talks about Iraq, at least, not to me. He is no longer stuck in the desert, in 110-degree temperatures. His world is no longer filled with moon dust, the fine, silky silt that gets into truck gears, the magazines of rifles, and under eyelids. Mauro has moved beyond Iraq, but I am still there, ensnared in the Iraq of my imagination. Who knows if I'll ever be free?

Imagining Iraq

He spoke in a monotone, as though reciting a prayer learned in childhood, and he never looked me in the eye.

"We were in a little village outside of Al-Karmah," he began, "about sixteen klicks northeast of Fallujah. Karmah, ha! What a dumb name. It was the most violent city in Iraq."

"I thought that was Fallujah."

"This was worse. At least there's a wall around Fallujah. Here there was nothing. No protection at all. The bastards could walk right into town and attack our patrols. IEDs, mortar attacks, all that shit. We lost so many guys…" He fell into silence.

I sat there waiting. "Want some more coffee?" I asked finally.

"Nah… yeah, sure. Why not?"

I got up and took the pot off the stove.

He sipped his coffee slowly, as if reluctant to go on.

"Al-Karmah was an Al-Qaida stronghold, a tribal safe haven."

Another pause.

"After the Awakening—you know, when the Sunni sheiks finally decided to work with the Marines instead of Al-Qaida because Al-Qaida was too fucking violent—things changed. People started to report the smugglers. We'd go into these little villages, and the people would tell us where the weapons caches were. A lot of them had lost family members to Al-Qaida, see? Somebody didn't go along with what Al-Qaida wanted, and the next morning the head of one of their kids would show up on their doorstep. They were brutal bastards, Al-Qaida. They'd cut off kids' heads to intimidate their parents. I liked the Iraqi people well enough, the ones I met, but the terrorists, I never felt an ounce of regret about taking one of those guys out."

It was the longest snatch of language I'd heard from him since he'd moved in, and the first time I'd heard him swear. Corey Frater almost never talked, and when he did, he was polite and soft-spoken. If he said *damn* or even *jerk*, he excused himself first. "The guy was… excuse me, ma'am… but the guy was a real jerk."

I'd had a room to let, and he answered my ad. I liked him right away. A brawny young vet with blond hair, impenetrable blue eyes, and a square jaw, he reminded me of the men in the recruiting advertisements: "The few. The proud. The Marines." And he reminded me of my son Ignacio.

"Naturally," I said. "That was your job: to stop Al-Qaida."

"Yeah," he said. "To stop Al-Qaida."

He slouched down in his chair. His jaw tightened slightly, and I didn't know whether he was going to go on. The aroma of coffee filled the kitchen, giving the place a warm, cozy feel, but I knew he was a million miles away, in some godforsaken village on the outskirts of the inappropriately named city of Al-Karmah.

"It's actually a beautiful place," he said abruptly. He laughed. "When the sunlight glimmers on the river, it's breathtaking. Parts of the Tigris-Euphrates valley are so green. It's where the Garden of Eden was. Sometimes I thought, if I have to die over here, this is a good place."

A frisson shot up my arm. I wondered if my son had ever had that same thought.

"Sometimes we parachuted in. We'd sneak into a village at night to gather information. But that day we went in by truck. We made a lot of noise, too much noise. There were six of us—five Marines and a terp... you know... an interpreter, named Hakim. Except for the part that's irrigated, it's all sand. Sand everywhere. A great big sandbox. We called it moon dust. It was so fine and silty that it got into everything—under your nails, into your nose, into your skin. You had to be careful it didn't get into the engine because it could wreck your truck. We had to change air filters all the time." He fidgeted with a napkin and then sipped his coffee.

"We were supposed to move in for a few days and scout around. Who was with us, who was against, that sort of thing. We had intelligence that there'd been some insurgent sympathizers in the village and that they'd hidden weapons somewhere. A favorite place was the school. If there were bombs in a school, you didn't want to go in because then they'd set them off and kill a bunch of kids. They knew the Americans didn't want civilian casualties, especially not children, so that's where they'd hide their hardware, the bastards."

I scrutinized his face for traces of anger, but in spite of his harsh words, he appeared composed.

Suddenly he sprang up. "I'm sorry, ma'am. I shouldn't be bothering you with this."

"You're not bothering me at all," I countered. "It's interesting. Please go on."

He hesitated, nodded, and then shrugged.

I wondered what he was thinking. It was obvious he didn't like to talk about the war. Before then, I had no idea where he'd been, what he'd done. Now I learned that he was a staff sergeant, a recon guy in charge of a small team of Marines, and a master freefall parachutist. His specialty was dropping in behind enemy lines in the dead of night to gather intelligence with all kinds of fancy surveillance equipment.

"Have some more coffee, Corey," I said, getting up. "I have some blueberry muffins too. Want one?" I didn't want him to stop talking. My own son had never told me anything at all about the war, and I was ravenous for information. I opened a package of muffins and put them on a plate, wondering what it would feel like to jump out of a plane at 29,000 feet. Does your stomach float up to your throat? Are you terrified your chute won't open? Can you breathe normally? I speculated about whether Ignacio had ever plunged into enemy territory that way. I thought not. He was an infantry Marine. He strode up to a house and kicked in the door. At least, that was my understanding of things.

"This time we didn't parachute in," he said, as though reading my thoughts. "Of the five Americans, Jake was the only one who hadn't done this gig before, and he made me a little nervous. The rest of us, including Hakim, had been together for weeks. Each guy knew his job and everybody else's. Unless we met with resistance and got into a firefight or something like that, these operations usually went off like clockwork—especially now that the Sunnis were mostly cooperating. It was Jake's fault we made too much noise. I told him to slow the motor, to cool it, but he was determined to roar into town: 'We're Americans and we're here to save you!' That kind of shit. I was afraid he'd frighten the folks and cause bad feelings."

"Did he?"

"Yes, but not with the Humvee."

He sat for a moment staring into space, lost in the depths of his memory.

"Another muffin, Corey?"

He blinked and started, as though awakening from a trance.

"A man came out to meet us. He was one of the village elders. In a community like that, a stranger draws attention. Hakim explained our mission to him and told him we'd be there for a few days. We were gathering information, and we needed a base of operations. Could he find us a house?"

I imagined the elder: a wizened old man

with shrewd ferret eyes in a brown, lackluster face. I imagined him wearing a long, colorless *dishdasha* and a red and white checked *keffiyeh*—the kind of headdress Arab men wear to protect themselves from the sun. (I knew what a *keffiyeh* was because Ignacio had emailed me pictures.) I conjured up the man's small but sturdy frame, his leathery skin, his dusty sandals, his gnarled hands reeking of sheep dung and aniseed. He stood enveloped in the implacable Iraqi sunlight against a blue, motionless sky, bereft of even a single languorous cloud. Ribbons of light reached out of the heavens and splintered into the distant Euphrates. I had spent years imagining Iraq, wondering what it was like to tread that silty sand under the relentless, blazing sun, carrying sixty pounds of gear on my back, plus weapons. My son had done it. Corey had done it. And with a mother's obsessiveness, I had created and recreated in my mind the experiences I thought they had lived through. But, of course, I couldn't know what it was like… not at all, not really.

"Was he angry, the elder?"

"He didn't seem angry. He showed us to the home of his son, Ali. He thought it would be appropriate for our needs, he said."

"His own son? How generous. He must

have been on our side."

"By then, most of the Sunni sheiks were."

I hesitated. "Can you tell me what the house looked like?" I was afraid that if I asked too many questions, he would shut down again, and maybe this time he'd refuse to go on.

"It was pretty large for a rural house, but then, Ali was the son of an elder. When you went through the front door, you found yourself in a sizeable main room. That was the plan of most of the houses. Off to the sides were the kitchen and bedrooms. You could access the main room from any part of the house. There were no doors. Americans think privacy is a big deal, but Iraqis don't. The floors were concrete and there was almost no furniture. People sit on the floor to eat, the men first, and then the women and children. We looked around and decided the place was perfect for us. I asked Hashim to thank Ali and his father and promised we'd take good care of everything.

"Of course, Jake had to go and say something stupid. 'Nice digs for a bunch of towel-heads,' he said. There was another guy, Dave, a radio operator. He turned around to Jake and snapped, 'Shut up, you moron.' He'd taken a dislike to Jake from the beginning."

"Did you meet the family?"

"They were all there: Ali, his wife Farrah, and four children. Ali was the one who talked to us, of course. He came out to greet us with his two little boys. I guess they were about nine and six or seven. The wife and two little girls stayed in the kitchen. The tiniest one—she couldn't have been more than three—hid behind a barrel and peeped out at us. She was the cutest little thing, with enormous brown eyes, puffy cheeks, and a captivating smile. Her name was Leyla. I wanted to pick her up and squeeze her. She and her sister, who was about five, would catch my glance and burst into giggles. I wished I had a teddy bear or something to give her. I put my hand in my pocket and found some candy—we always carried candy to hand out to the children—and the older girl tiptoed out of the kitchen and took it from me. Then she turned around and scampered back, shrieking with laughter."

Corey was smiling broadly. For a moment he had abandoned his reserve and let himself go. But then he drifted back into melancholy.

"It was a sheepherding area, and all the men were shepherds, so of course they had a dog. It was out in the pen, a beautiful herder, tan and black with huge brown intelligent eyes. It looked as though it were smiling at us. Iraqis don't usually get sentimental about pets the way we do, but a shepherd needs his dog, and Ali clearly loved this one. The family was going to vacate the house for us—they would be staying with cousins—but they were going to have to leave the dog behind. I never caught what his name was, but we called him Raj.

"David said we could feed him our MREs, since that's all that military grub was good for anyway. We all laughed, but then Jake made a crack about using the dog for target practice. Dave was really getting pissed. 'Shut the fuck up, you asshole,' he snapped. I'm sorry, ma'am, but that's the way Marines talk."

"That must have been awful for the family! Imagine having to hand over your house to a bunch of foreign soldiers."

Corey sighed. "I know. I felt terrible about it. And they were so gracious. Imagine, before they left, Farrah spent hours cooking. She left us enough food for a week! Even meat! And, you know, meat is a luxury."

I imagined Farrah, invisible under her long *abaya*, her head covered with a *hijab*, scurrying around her kitchen to prepare food for foreigners, only to have to abandon her house afterward.

"'Don't worry about the dog,' I told Ali

when they left. 'We'll take care of him.' Little Leyla gave me a big smile and stuffed a fig into my hand. 'I think she likes you,' Ali told me. He said it in fractured English, laughing."

Corey took a sip of coffee.

"It must be cold," I said. "I'll get you a new one."

He shook his head. "Please don't bother, ma'am. Cold coffee's not the worst thing I've ever dealt with."

"Of course not, but…"

He wasn't listening. He'd slipped back into gloom. His dejection wasn't perceptible in his eyes or his mouth, but only in that slight tightening of the jaw—and the silence.

Suddenly I felt embarrassed. I had urged him to talk out of… what? Greed. Greed for what? Vicarious experience. I ached to know what I could never know: what it was like to be there. I'd been selfish, and I felt contrite.

"You don't have to go on," I said softly. "I can see it brings back bad memories."

He turned to me and shrugged. "No big deal," he said in that offhanded tone soldiers use when they try to convince you that something truly horrific hasn't affected them. "No big deal." The stoics. The real men. The tough guys. The few, the proud, the Marines. Ignacio used that tone too, when his best friend and future housemate got blown to smithereens by an IED.

"After they left, the dog became restless." Corey was clearly determined to finish the story. "He missed them, and he didn't like that strange people were living in the house.

"Dave went out to calm him down. 'It's okay, Raj,' he kept saying. 'Come on, Raj, let's play ball!' But we didn't have a ball, so he threw a stick instead. 'Go ahead, Raj! Go fetch it.' Gradually Raj got into it. He ran after the stick and brought it back a couple of times. Dave and I gave him some MREs and roared with laughter when he gobbled them up. Dave snickered. 'See?' he said. 'I told you that stuff wasn't fit for human consumption!'

"At dusk Raj grew distressed again. He paced and barked and whined. He knew something was wrong. Ali hadn't taken him out with the sheep, and the family hadn't come back from wherever they were. By nightfall the dog was miserable. 'Shut that fucking dog up or none of us will get any sleep,' Jake kept complaining. 'Put a blanket over your head, asshole,' Dave fired back.

"But by the third night, all of us were frazzled. Raj had a sharp bark that pierced you like a bullet, and his whining sounded like the howl of a coyote. He was driving everybody nuts, even Dave. All night long he yapped and yowled.

"But then, suddenly, the barking stopped.

"When I got up the next morning and went out to the pen, there was Raj, dead, lying in a brown pool of blood. Jake had put a silencer on his gun and gone out and shot him."

Corey's voice quivered slightly, and his eyes looked faintly swollen.

"I opened the pen and stood there looking at that poor animal, the one we'd promised to take care of. 'What the hell's the matter with you, you idiot?' I said to Jake. 'Why'd you have to go and kill the fucking dog? These people were nice to us! This could have been a productive experience, man. Winning hearts and minds and all that crap, remember?'

"Jake just stood there with a warped grin on his face. Suddenly, Dave flew at him with a snarl. He punched him in the jaw so hard I thought he'd kill him. Jake stumbled and then went crashing into the sand. For a moment he didn't move. But then he pulled himself up. He gawked at us awhile and then burst out laughing. He just roared with laughter. His whole body was covered with blood and dog shit."

Corey pursed his lips and looked blankly

at the opposite wall. "I'm sorry, ma'am. I shouldn't have told you. I don't know why I did."

I longed to reach out and squeeze his hand, but I knew better.

"It's just that... It was such a lovely family. They were so friendly, so anxious to cooperate. And then the fucking moron... sorry, ma'am... and then Jake goes and kills their dog."

I sensed his rage, even as he struggled to regain his stoic demeanor.

"Thanks for the coffee, ma'am." He stood up, took his cup to the sink, and washed it, careful to keep his back toward me the whole time.

I grasped then what I hadn't before: Raj was the whole war—the lost buddies, the wailing children, the sudden explosions followed by intense darkness, the sirens in the night. Raj was the senseless death of innocents and the tears shed in secret by so many soldiers—Corey, Dave, Ignacio... all of them. Raj was the Iraq I just couldn't fathom, just couldn't imagine, no matter how hard I tried.

A Lucky Son of a Bitch

"High cheekbones. Tight jaw. A big black motherfucker with a permanent scowl. We knew from the beginning that Sergeant Edmunds wasn't going to take any crap from a pack of nineteen-year-olds like us, but every once in a while, you wanted to push the envelope. That's just how guys are."

He fiddled with his checkbook as if he were waiting for permission to continue. "Too bad you can't take a credit card, ma'am," he mumbled.

"You know I can't take a card for the rent, Eb. I told you, a personal check the first of the month, and make sure this one doesn't bounce."

He looked at me forlornly. "I'm sorry about last month, ma'am. It won't happen again."

He slouched on the kitchen chair, turning the checkbook over and over. He was taciturn by nature—although I'd seen him cut up with the other boarders a couple of times. Always late at night, after a couple of beers.

I'd started renting out rooms after my son

Ignacio left for basic training—nearly always to veterans returning from Iraq or Afghanistan. It helped fill the void. Sometimes they'd tell me stories, and certain scenes lodged in my brain—the blinding desert aglow with reflected sunlight, sweat-soaked bodies atop a rusty truck, a burka-clad woman coddling a simmering lamb stew redolent with cumin and coriander, children crouching in terror, missiles whirring. I knew I could never capture Ignacio's reality in my mind but hearing the boarders' tales made me feel closer to him.

"Go on," I prodded. "Sergeant Edmunds was a large man, an African-American."

"No, ma'am." He sighed and stared at the checkbook, as if the rest of the story were written on the "Pay to the Order of" line. He seemed to have forgotten I was there.

"He wasn't African-American?" I said after a while.

"The base was outside of Fallujah," he said finally. "We knew we were going in soon, but nobody knew when. It must have been at least 110 degrees in the shade that day. Drops were collecting on Sergeant Edmunds's brow, but no one paid much attention. We were all oozing like pigs.

"'Langston!' Edmunds barked at me.

'Your shoelace is untied!'

"'Yeah, okay,'" I said. "I crouched down to fasten it. Edmunds was hanging over me like some kind of a fucking Goliath."

"'What did you say, son?' Edmunds said.

"I corrected myself: 'Yes, Sergeant.'

"She was a staff sergeant, and as the only female on the base, she claimed certain privileges. You had to show her respect. Otherwise, she'd get mad, and you really didn't want to have Sergeant Edmunds mad at you, because she could make your life a living hell. She could give you all the shit work—literally. I mean, cleaning latrines and crap like that."

"You mean Sergeant Edmunds was a *woman*?!"

"She certainly was. A tall, curvaceous woman with long, beautiful legs. Well, I imagine they were beautiful. I never got to see them, of course. But from where I squatted in the dirt that day, her legs looked like telephone poles wrapped in camouflage. Up, up, up they went, unending, until they reached… her torso."

I smiled. I imagined him crouching in the sand before the majestic Sergeant Edmunds, struggling to tie his laces and simultaneously catch a surreptitious glimpse of her crotch.

When Ebenezer Langston appeared at my door asking to rent a room, I almost said no. Even though he didn't use a crutch or a cane, I could tell he was missing a leg. I could see the prosthesis sticking out from his pants. He didn't seem like a very promising tenant, this young, wounded, unemployed veteran. And then there was the aftershave—the heady, herbaceous scent of lavender and coumarin that followed him everywhere. No, I thought. The cologne alone will drive me to distraction.

But then, he looked me straight in the eye and said, "You know, I don't have to take a desk job. I can do anything. I'm very mobile. Just because I lost a limb doesn't mean I can't perform physical labor." He lifted his jean leg to the knee and pointed to the contraption. "This doesn't slow me up a bit. It takes me longer to comb my hair in the morning than it does to put on my leg."

How could I not take him in after that? He was so determined, so earnest. I'll get used to the cologne, I thought. I gave him the bedroom that had once been my sewing room.

"So…" I began gingerly, "you were fond of Sergeant Edmunds."

"Are you kidding? I hated her."

"But you said she was beautiful."

"She was an engineer, the only woman on

a base of two hundred men. A demolitions expert specializing in urban breaching and landmines. She could destroy anything; most of all, your self-confidence. She was tall, probably over six feet, and she had a glare that could melt metal. When she looked at you with those unblinking black eyes, you flinched, even if you were an older, experienced Marine. Which I wasn't. I was a nineteen-year-old kid right out of high school, and I hated her."

"'You know something, Langston?' she said to me one morning. 'You stink. There's always one stinky kid in every unit, and in this one, it's you.'

"I didn't say anything.

"'Do you know that you stink, Langston? Can you smell yourself? You have body odor so bad it makes me gag. Do you ever take a shower?'

"I wanted to kill her. I'm not kidding. At that moment, I wanted to put a bullet right between her eyes. After that, the guys started calling me Stinky. It was 'Stinky, give me a cigarette,' and 'Stinky, throw me a rag.' Fucking bitch. She made me the butt of everyone's jokes. 'White boy,' one of the guys said to me, 'you stink so bad my mamma's asshole smells like vanilla ice cream compared with you.' I vowed that when I got out—*if* I got out—nobody would ever call me Stinky again. That's why I always wear aftershave."

"Uh," I said as delicately as possible, "about the aftershave…"

"Nice, isn't it?" He blushed and grinned in a hangdog way.

"I… uh… sure. It's just that…"

"It's the only luxury I spend money on," he confided.

"Sure, Eb," I said. "It's very nice."

"Anyway," he went on, "Edmunds kept on teasing me. 'Hey, kid, where'd you get the name Ebenezer?' she asked one day while I was cleaning my rifle.

"My dad's a preacher," I mumbled. "He gave us all biblical names.

"'Yeah? Ain't nothing biblical about you, sewer-stink,' she growled. 'And be careful with that gun. It's a weapon, for God's sake. It's supposed to keep you safe. Make sure you get all the sand out of it.' I was wiping off the lower receiver with a rag, lubricating the metal carefully, but the way she was talking, you'd have thought I was flipping it in the air without checking the safety. I could feel the blood rushing to my temples. Suddenly, I blurted out, 'Where'd you get the name Missy, Sarge?'

"She wheeled around and glared at me. 'What?'

"'That's your name, right, Sarge? Missy Edmunds? Only there ain't nothing missy about you. You're about as missy as I am biblical.'

"'It's Melissa,' she hissed. I expected her to shoot venom right through my skull with her glare. Instead she just turned and walked away.

"That evening the order came. We had intelligence that some civilians were harboring Al-Qaida, including two or three HVTs—high-value targets. Nasty men. Men who put bombs in marketplaces and schools. We were charged with taking the house and, if possible, capturing these guys alive. If we did, they'd be an information gold mine. It would be hard though. They were heavily armed and had intelligence networks of their own."

I tried to imagine what it would be like to be headed into that nest of brutality. You knew the first guy in the door would get shot. You had to be afraid it might be you.

I wondered if Ignacio had ever been to Fallujah. If he had, he wouldn't tell me, of course. He never told me where he was or what he was doing. That's why the boarders' stories were so important to me. I was struggling to understand the reality Ignacio was living, and all I had to go on was what I read in the newspapers and the tales of these reticent young men, who on rare occasions opened up and talked to me.

"We had detailed maps of Fallujah and, of course, plans of the house," Eb was saying. "I was nervous, ma'am, I admit it. I stood in the yard and looked at the sky. What if this is the last sunset I ever see in my life? I thought. I went into the shop to get some screws, but I wasn't thinking clearly. I lit a cigarette and took a couple of steps. Suddenly, Jezebel was all over me."

"You mean Edmunds?"

"Of course I mean Edmunds. 'You moron!' she screamed. 'Put out that fucking cigarette! Don't you know better than to light a match around fuel? You are an idiot, Langston! You're a danger to the whole operation. You're no Marine! You don't deserve to wear that uniform! Go back to the fucking Boy Scouts! You're so dumb that if you were a dog, you'd probably try to mount a bitch from the head side!' On and on she went."

His tone was fierce as he related the details.

"She grabbed my wrist and yanked away the cigarette. She had a grip like a vise.

"I glowered at her and took off toward the tools. 'Cunt!' I whispered under my breath."

He looked up at me. "Sorry ma'am," he said, "but you have to understand, I was hopping mad."

He paused a second, and then went on. "I thought I'd said it too low for her to hear, but she had ears like a bat's. Suddenly, she was right behind me, so close I could feel her breasts graze my shoulders. 'What was that, Langston?' she snarled.

"'I didn't say anything,' I whispered. She seized my arm. I thought she would squeeze all the juice out of me.

"'Yes, you did, asshole,' she hissed. 'Repeat it!'

"The guys were all looking at me. 'Go ahead and tell her what you said, Stinky,' teased one of them—a lanky kid from Tennessee who was always looking for fun.

"'Yeah, tell her!' hooted another one. 'What difference does it make if she kills you? Tomorrow we're all gonna die anyway.'

"I was already scared," Eb told me, "and that talk about dying pushed me over the brink. 'Shut the fuck up!' I screamed.

"Sergeant Edmunds was still standing

there, arms crossed, hellfire in her eyes. 'Repeat it,' she said slowly, as if she were speaking to a doltish schoolboy.

"Suddenly, I twirled around and hurled the word at her: 'Cunt!' I screamed. 'I called you a cunt!'"

"Before I saw Sergeant Edmunds lift her fist I felt a searing pain in the jaw. It was as though someone had scorched my face with a branding iron," Ebenezer said, holding his cheek as though it still hurt. "The room was reeling. I could hear the guys snickering and taunting: 'He got beat up by a broad!' I teetered and slumped to the ground.

"'Get up, asshole!' snarled Edmunds. 'We don't have time for this. We're getting ready for a raid, or hadn't you heard?'"

They moved out in the middle of the night. "There were six or eight trucks," explained Eb. "We had infrared and ammo and all the tools we needed, but there wasn't a guy who wasn't thinking about his girlfriend, his wife, his mother, or his kids, and the chance that he'd never see them again. The moon reminded me of an enormous candied lemon, and I wondered how it had the gall to look so luscious when honorable young men from Tennessee and Montana and Georgia were about to spill their blood in its filmy beams. My jaw was swollen, but I couldn't think about it then. I had to push Sergeant Edmunds and her vicious temper out of my mind. I had to focus on the mission at hand. I had to be tough.

"'The Lord is my shepherd.' I mouthed the words silently. 'Though I walk through the valley of the shadow of death, I will fear no evil...' I did fear evil though, and God seemed very far away.

"And yet... I don't know how to explain it, ma'am." Ebenezer was looking at me with his huge, earnest eyes. A lock of sandy-brown hair had fallen across his brow. "It's the adrenaline. You feel pumped. You know you might die, but you can't wait to get there. It's weird."

I smiled. I was tired. I had to get up the next morning for work, yet I wanted him to keep talking. I was thinking about Ignacio, imagining him in a truck on the way to some hellhole in the middle of the night.

"Yes," I whispered. "Weird."

"We were creeping along. It was so quiet we could hear our own breathing. Nobody talked. Everyone knew that this road was one of Al-Qaida's favorites for planting bombs. And yet, in the light of that lemon-drop moon, you hardly believed that anything bad could happen. It just didn't seem like the right place to die.

"But every place is the right place to die for someone.

"I can't remember exactly what happened next. Someone shoved me out of the truck. 'What the hell!' I remember screaming. Then, a flash, a blaze, and everything went dark. I mean, totally black. It was the blackest black I'd ever experienced—like being somewhere in the earth's bowels. I felt a thud and smelled smoke and something like burning meat. I recall hearing a confused clamor—cries, sirens, shots. I thought I was blind... or dead. Then suddenly, I felt myself moving, flying, transported through the air by some extraordinary force. No pain, just a sensation of soaring. It lasted only a moment, and then everything went blank.

"I woke up in a hospital in Baghdad. A Navy doctor and a nurse were fussing around me. It was hard for me to understand what they were saying. My head was throbbing, and the words seemed to ooze together, but after a while I grasped that they were going to fly me to Germany. I must be dying, I thought. Landstuhl Medical Center is where they send soldiers to die. I blinked and made out the outline of the woman standing by my bed. She was taking my pulse and looking distractedly out the window. I grunted.

"'Ah,' she said. 'You're awake. Finally.'

"'I need to get back to my unit,' I whispered.

"She smiled and popped a thermometer into my mouth. 'You're one of the lucky ones,' she said finally.

"That's all she said. It wasn't until much later that I found out what had happened." Eb bit his lip and peered at me from under that unruly shock of hair. "The two guys in the front of the truck were blown to bits," he whispered. He rubbed his chin to keep his jaw from quivering. I could almost hear the voice in his head urging him to keep calm, to be tough. "But the vehicle separated grotesquely in the middle, and the guys in the back survived."

He sighed.

"She saved me," he said finally.

"The nurse?"

"No, ma'am. Not the nurse. Missy. She shoved me out of the truck right before the worst of it. Of all the guys who made it, I suffered the fewest injuries. I lost a leg, but they lost... more."

The evening light had softened his features, giving them an almost cherubic sweetness. His cheeks still had the ruddy glow of a child's. I was suddenly aware of how young he was. Twenty-three or twenty-four—a boy, really. Ignacio was only twenty-seven, but his angular features gave him a more mature appearance. I had tears in my eyes and had to look away.

"She pushed me out and carried me away from the blast. I was bleeding like a butchered pig. I could have bled to death. But she bandaged me up the best she could, then got me back to base. From there, they flew me by medevac to Baghdad."

"The evil Sergeant Edmunds…"

"When I was in rehab at Walter Reed, she came to see me. She'd left the military by then. She was wearing jeans and a tight red sweater, and she looked… well… sexy." He laughed and blushed. "We joked around, and I promised her that I'd never be stinky again, that the minute I was well enough, I'd buy cologne and smell like… I don't know… jasmine or lavender… whatever that stuff is made out of. It was a beautiful warm day. Sunlight glimmered through the trees—nothing like that blistering Iraqi sunlight that leaves you debilitated and depressed, but soft, welcoming rays like on the day God delivered Noah from the flood. I hobbled around the grounds with her. Her skin was so smooth, so moist—like glistening chocolate."

"You're very poetic, Eb."

He blushed again and withdrew into silence.

"What happened to her? Are you still in touch?"

"No, not really. She's married."

"Really? Who'd she marry?"

"Some asshole." He laughed. "He's a vice president at the bank where she works. What a lucky son of a bitch!"

Eb pulled himself up and handed me a check.

"Thanks, Ebenezer," I said. "Good night."

"'Night, ma'am. And don't worry. This one won't bounce."

The Call

Every time Cándida López saw a strange car in the street, she reviewed in her mind the most efficient ways to commit suicide. If Riqui were dead, two Marines would knock on her door and recite some canned speech, the same speech they always gave when they told a mother her child had made "the ultimate sacrifice." Then they'd go out and have a beer. And what about the mother? Pills, thought Cándida. Just drop off to sleep and never wake up. Or carbon monoxide. "Too bad I don't know how to use a gun," she said out loud.

But what if Riqui were injured? There would be a call, probably from some hospital in Baghdad or the medical center in Landstuhl. A lot of the guys airlifted to Landstuhl never made it home alive. Or else they came back too battered to lead normal lives. She'd read all about it in *La Opinión*.

The doctor had told her to stop reading the news, stop watching Univisión, stop listening to the radio, but she was addicted. She checked the Net ten, maybe twelve times a day. Whenever a bomb went off or a plane went down, she knelt on the floor and prayed.

"Please, Holy Virgin, don't let it be Riqui," she'd whisper.

"What's the point of checking the news?" her friend Carolyn chided. "All it does is upset you."

"I know," sighed Cándida. She felt enchained in a prison of helplessness.

"I heard about a grandmother who joined the Army," she told Riqui before he left. "She went over to Iraq to cook for the troops to be near her grandson. What if I did that?"

"Forget it, Mom!"

"Riqui…" Cándida felt as though a rough-edged stone were lodged in her throat. "You're my only son, my only child…"

"Everything will be fine, Mom. The guys all protect each other."

"*Dios te oiga, hijo.* I hope God is listening."

The phone rang. Cándida flinched. She stood there staring at the black object hanging on the wall as though it were a dead rat.

Finally, she picked up the receiver. "Hello?" she said.

"Hey, Cándida. It's Carolyn. You okay?"

Cándida exhaled in relief.

* * *

When she'd left El Salvador in 1985, the

civil war was raging. The FMLA was ambushing anyone with a cow or a radio and putting a gun to his head. Private property was evil, they said. Whatever you had belonged to the revolution.

"We don't have to worry," insisted Cándida's husband Ricardo. "We don't have anything they want." But he was wrong.

One night, as Cándida was putting the children to bed, she felt strangely uneasy. Suddenly, an explosion sent her reeling. There were only two rooms in the miniscule house, the bedroom and an all-purpose room for cooking, eating, and everything else. That's the room that had a door, and someone had shot it open.

"Hide!" she ordered.

Riqui, then three, dove under the cot, but it was too late for eleven-year-old Nélida. The soldiers—a gang of ragtag thugs who called themselves guerrillas—were already in the room. One of them grabbed the girl and pulled off her dress, while the others threw Cándida to the floor. Then they undid their pants and took turns.

When Ricardo got back from his Uncle Raúl's house, the first thing he noticed was that the chicken coop was empty. He stopped in his tracks and scrutinized the yard. Feathers and eggshells and human feces were strewn everywhere. Ricardo's temples started to throb and his fingers turned icy. The door to the house had been blasted to pieces. The pots and pans that normally hung on the wall were missing.

He found his wife hysterical and writhing with pain. His inert daughter was sprawled out in a pool of blood. Cándida was babbling something—boys, rape, *Virgen María*. He couldn't make out the words, but he'd already grasped what had happened. Next to Nélida lay a shattered, bloodied statue of the Holy Mother. It had been the only object of beauty in the house. They'd smashed it over Neli's head, probably to silence her, or maybe just for fun.

Ricardo crumpled. Their beautiful child— her wide, tiger eyes; her smooth brown skin; her full lips and budding body.

They buried her in the village cemetery. Ricardo held little Riqui in his arms and watched his uncles and cousins lower the casket into the ground. He was a poor, insignificant man, but he wasn't going to let those brutes get away with this crime.

"I'm going to join the army," he vowed. "I'll take care of them."

"The government soldiers are just as

brutal as the guerrillas," countered his cousin Juan. "What you need to do is get out of here. Find a coyote who'll sneak you through Mexico and over the U.S. border."

"Who has money for a coyote?"

"We could pool our resources."

"How much could all of us put together? Coyotes charge three or four hundred dollars a head." Ricardo inhaled on his foul-smelling cigarette.

"At least enough for Cándida and Riqui," said Uncle Raúl. "Or if not, you can borrow money from Tello. He's financed a lot of people. They pay him back once they get there. I hear you can make forty or fifty dollars a day in the U.S. A day! Imagine! You'll be able to pay Tello back in a couple of months!"

Tello was the owner of the only store in the village of San Teófanes. He sold everything from chicken feed to beer to ladies' panties.

Uncle Raúl lit a cigarette with trembling hands. His skin was as fragile and crinkled as a used paper bag and his fingers, as knotted as ropes. But his mind was sharp. Ricardo was listening.

"You owe it to your son. You have to get him out of here."

"What if they get caught?"

"The coyotes know all the secret routes. After Cándida gets settled, you can follow."

"Holy Virgin," moaned Cándida. But she knew Uncle Raúl was right.

* * *

She crossed the border stuffed into the hidden compartment of a truck, her son tucked under her. The driver put them on a bus to Los Angeles, where a Salvadoran woman named Vilma, who routinely scoured the station for newcomers, offered them a room for $100 a month.

"I don't have that kind of money," Cándida told her.

"You will," said Vilma.

The barrio streets were strewn with garbage, and the walls covered with lurid graffiti. Everywhere men who reminded her of the hooligans who had raped her and Neli hung around smoking and spewing obscenities. They made her shudder.

Vilma got her a job in a restaurant washing dishes. Riqui went too, because she had nowhere to leave him. At night, she attended English classes at the local church. That's where she met an Ethiopian woman named Aisha who told her about a family in Beverly Hills that was looking for a live-in nanny.

"Get out of this neighborhood before it's too late," said Aisha. "Before the gangs get to your boy."

"He's just a baby."

"Exactly. There's still time."

Cándida had just escaped from a war zone, but the barrio was a war zone too. She took the nanny job.

"Stay in touch!" said Vilma when Cándida moved out. "Come eat tamales and *pupusa*s with me on Sundays."

"I will," Cándida assured her.

And she did. She wasn't in the least homesick for San Teófanes, but she loved the familiar aromas of Vilma's kitchen. She loved hearing her local dialect and catching up on news. Vilma's little group gave her a sense of community in this new and alien country.

Beverly Hills was like some sort of fantasy—blocks and blocks of manicured lawns, soaring palm trees and crimson oleanders, driveways with exotic automobiles. Janine McGovern, Cándida's employer, was an attorney with too much to do, so it was up to Cándida to get the children off to school and care for the house. She and Riqui had their own room with a bathroom and a toilet that flushed. Before long, Riqui was in a neighborhood school free of marauding gangs. Everything would be fine, thought Cándida, as long as she could stay out of sight of the immigration authorities—*la migra*—and didn't do something stupid like apply for refugee status. Mrs. McGovern had told her that less than three percent of the Central Americans who applied got it. By applying, you only attracted attention to yourself.

"Sorry," she said. "Even though I'm a lawyer, I can't help."

In two years Cándida had learned passable English. "Don' forget you mat' book!" she called to David, Mrs. McGovern's ten-year-old son, when he left for school.

She took a second job in a little beauty shop on Beverly Boulevard, shampooing the heads of elegant ladies, on Saturdays. She needed the extra money. She was saving up to bring Ricardo to Los Angeles. It was at the beauty shop that she met Carolyn, a beautician with frizzy blond hair and a heart of gold beating under an enormous bosom.

Every month, Cándida sent a money order to Tello to pay off her debt, and another one to Uncle Raúl to ease his burdens. Uncle Raúl couldn't write, but Tello occasionally sent a note with news from the community. Juan's wife had just had a baby girl. Raúl had bought a cow and two goats that he watched like toddlers. Ricardo had joined the army, and no one had seen him in months. Cándida went to church and lit a candle for her husband.

"Virgen," she prayed, "even though they abused you in our house, please don't abandon us."

Eventually the letters stopped coming. By now Cándida had paid off the debt to Tello, but she was still sending money orders for Uncle Raúl. She tried to call—telephone service was now available in San Teófanes—but no one ever answered.

She explained the problem to Vilma, who promised to ask around.

It took a few weeks, during which Cándida prayed a lot and cried a lot. When the answer finally came, it was devastating. Government troops had overrun San Teófanes, ransacked Tello's store, stolen Raúl's animals, and shot everyone but the few folks who had managed to flee. Now there were phones, but no one to answer them.

"And Ricardo?"

"Nothing about Ricardo."

"He might be dead."

"He might be," said Vilma matter-of-factly. "After all, it's a war."

"I will never, ever let my son go to war," said Cándida.

* * *

By 1992 the conflict in El Salvador was over. Thousands of Salvadorans headed back home, but Cándida decided to stay put. She'd left Mrs. McGovern a couple of years before. Carolyn had convinced her to study for her high school equivalency diploma and a beautician's license. Standing over fussy ladies for hours at a time, mixing dye, combing curls, remembering who had just gotten a divorce and who'd vacationed on the Riviera was exhausting, but Cándida didn't complain. She had a little apartment in Santa Monica and a used Toyota. If only it weren't for *la migra*, she could relax. But *la migra* was a constant worry. What if they popped into the beauty shop and dragged off all the illegals? It would be a nightmare for her, of course, but also for the owner, who had been kind to her. And what about Riqui, now in fifth grade and more gringo than *guanaco*?

One day in 1997, Mrs. McGovern called her. There had been a terrible earthquake in Central America, and the U.S. government had passed a relief act allowing undocumented Nicaraguans and Salvadorans to stay in the country.

"Now I can get you a green card," said Mrs. McGovern.

"Well," said Cándida to herself, "I've been through my own personal earthquake, so maybe I qualify."

"Any news about Ricardo?" added Mrs. McGovern.

"No, ma'am. Nothing."

* * *

Cándida had just gotten up and turned on the radio when the blaring voice of the newscaster announced that a plane had rammed into the World Trade Center in New York. Cándida assumed some amateur pilot had swiped the wall. *"Idiota!"* she said out loud.

She switched to the music station, where they were playing *"Ni tú ni nadie."* Cándida hummed along, lost in her calculations of Riqui's school expenses—he had just begun classes at Santa Monica College. Suddenly, an announcer interrupted. A second plane had flown into one of the towers, he said, and a third was headed for Washington, D.C.

Cándida felt her stomach tighten. She remembered things. A presentiment of danger. An explosion. Guerrilla thugs stomping through the house. Neli's screams.

The statue of the Virgin crashing to the floor. "No," she whispered. "No."

A few months later, she returned to the apartment to find Riqui in the living room with a Marine Corps recruiter. "Oh, God," moaned Cándida. "¿Qué es esto?"

Riqui had grown into a handsome boy. He'd have been tall in El Salvador, but here he was average height, about 5 feet 10 inches. He had the same tiger eyes as his sister, the same wide brow and smooth brown skin. His black hair draped over his forehead seductively. He grabbed a shock in his hand and smiled broadly at his mother.

"Take a good look, Mom, 'cause the next time you see me, I'll have a buzz cut!"

"You just started college, Riqui." She was struggling to stay calm.

"This country gave us a home, Mom. And now we're at war."

Cándida started to sob. "But we're not citizens," she said finally.

The recruiter, a tall black man with a no-nonsense demeanor, gazed over her head. "He's nineteen years old and a legal resident, ma'am. He can sign up."

The recruiter left. Riqui sat on the table, legs wide, eyes twinkling, already with that cocky Marine grin.

She had to admit she was proud. But she was also scared, so scared she felt nauseous.

"Listen, Mom," said Riqui, suddenly serious, "a long time ago… back there… you protected me. I couldn't defend you… or my sister." His voice was gentle. "But I'm never going to let anything bad happen to you again."

Cándida was still sobbing, and shivering like a sparrow in a winter wind.

"Look," said Riqui. "I'm going to show you something."

He went into his room and came back with a paper. Under the image of an eagle with outstretched wings were the words "U.S. Citizenship and Naturalization Services." He pointed to the text he had highlighted in yellow: "Special provisions of the Immigration and Nationality Act (INA) authorize U.S. Citizenship and Immigration Services (USCIS) to expedite the application and naturalization process for current members of the U.S. armed forces and recently discharged members."

"You see, Mom? If I serve, we can become citizens. No more worrying about *la migra* or renewing green cards."

"Don't do it for me, Riqui. I'd rather live in the shadows forever."

Days later the phone rang. When she thought about it afterward, it felt as though the whole scene had taken place in slow motion. It was the call she'd been expecting— and dreading. An official was calling from San Salvador. Ricardo was dead, he said. No details. That was the end of it.

Cándida steadied herself against the wall. Now her son was going off to war. Would there be another call someday? She had already lost her daughter and her husband. "Oh, Holy Virgin," she prayed, "watch over him."

The sleeplessness started even before Riqui left for boot camp. During the day, Cándida dozed on her feet. At night, she lay awake for hours, calculating Riqui's chances for survival. So far, only thirty-seven U.S. soldiers had died in Afghanistan. A tiny number. But if it was your kid who got hit... She started taking Excedrin PM—first one, then two, three, four. When she did fall into a fitful sleep, she dreamed of bombs and burning tanks. During the day, she contemplated suicide.

"Honey," said Carolyn, squeezing her shoulders, "you have to get some help." Furrows had formed over Carolyn's brow and around her eyes, and her chin had grown spongy. But her hair was still blond—she knew how to apply hair color, after all—and she was still as kind and caring as ever. Cándida thought she was lucky to have her for a friend.

The doctor wrote a prescription for Ambien, but it didn't help. In March 2003, the United States invaded Iraq, and in August, Riqui announced that he was being deployed. He was full of bravado. Lots of loud music and talk of kicking ass.

Carolyn became morose and obsessed with the news. She began to suffer from shortness of breath. She prayed, but found no relief. Gloom clung to her like an ugly black leech. Strangely, at the salon, no one but Carolyn knew anything was wrong. Cándida somehow kept up appearances, even though she felt as though she were suffocating.

Every day, she emailed Riqui. Weeks went by without a response.

"Sorry, Mom, I've been working," he explained when he finally called her. He made it sound as though he were shuffling papers at an insurance office.

It was late January 2004, and she hadn't heard from him since Christmas.

"They'll notify you right away if I'm dead," Riqui had joked. "If you don't get a call or a visit, don't worry."

Every time she heard about the death of an American soldier, she felt guilty because she felt relieved. It was a relief that it wasn't Riqui, but awful that some other woman just like her would be mourning.

She felt guilty about other things as well. Riqui had put his life at risk to protect her. To get her citizenship, so she'd never have to worry again about *la migra* or the green card. "Don't bother about me, Riqui," she whispered into the shadows. "Just stay alive."

One night she took more Ambien than she was supposed to, and then lay in bed staring into the dark.

The jangle of the telephone jolted her upright. A call in the middle of the night! She gasped for breath and clutched at the receiver.

"Hello?"

There was no one.

"Hello?"

Still, no one.

Cándida sat in the dark, hyperventilating. The digital clock with the bright green numbers read 1:32. Finally, she hung up.

She spent the rest of the night waiting for the phone to ring. "They'll call back," she told herself. But they didn't. The same feeling came over her as the day Vilma had told her that Ricardo was probably dead. She was certain, absolutely certain, that this would end the same way.

But then, after a month, Riqui called.

"Are you okay?" Cándida asked breathlessly. "The phone rang one night... I thought... something might have happened."

"No, nothing has happened." His voice sounded decisive.

They chatted a few minutes about nothing, and then Riqui asked suddenly, "When did you receive that call?"

"January... it must have been around the twenty-fifth. It was 1:32 in the morning. I'm certain about the hour."

Silence.

"*¿Hijo?*"

"No, nothing." He said goodbye and told her not to worry, the way he always did.

But Riqui knew what had happened on January 25. It was a day he would never forget. Lieutenant Metzer had sent him to a town outside of Ramadi rumored to be harboring an al-Qaida operative. His instructions were to observe what he could. He was to carry a military-issue cell phone with him to keep Metzer informed. He and four other Marines started out early in the morning, but right before they arrived, Riqui realized he didn't have the phone. He tried to remember where he'd left it. He thought back over the last few hours and recalled giving it to one of the Iraqi interpreters to make an authorized call. He thought the man had given it back, but now he wasn't sure.

At 11:32 a.m. — 1:32 a.m. in Los Angeles — Riqui López's phone set off a bomb in Ramadi that killed one Marine and left three critically injured. Riqui would have been a casualty too, if Metzer hadn't sent him on that mission. Riqui should have died that day. Somehow, the phone called his mother. How it happened, Riqui couldn't explain.

When Riqui left the Marines in 2006, the first thing he did was apply for U.S. citizenship. As soon as he got it, he could sponsor Cándida. One night, he took his mom out to dinner and told her the story about the phone.

Cándida felt as though the hand of God were stroking her cheek. "It was the Virgin calling to let me know you were okay," she said. "Only I didn't know how to interpret the message."

Riqui thought about how to respond. "Yeah, Mom," he said, biting into a tamale. "I'm sure that's it."

Judgment

Dan Lesko knew he would kill someone that morning.

He picked up his M40 and laid it gently on the table, along with a bore brush, a cleaning rod, and solvent. It's a painstaking operation, cleaning a gun. This one, a bolt-action sniper rifle, was Dan Lesko's sweetheart. It was more trustworthy, responsive, and predictable than any woman he had ever known. Sleek too. And beautiful. He stroked each part—the barrel, the stock. Then he massaged the scope with lens paper.

"Okay, honey," he said to the inert piece of metal and fiberglass. "We've got a job to do. Let's go do it."

The orders had come down the day before. Insurgents held a remote village on the outskirts of Rutbah, where they planned operations against Americans. Dan and his men had to flush them out, starting with their leader, Karim.

"It's like Fallujah," the captain had said. "Only smaller. The whole place is booby-trapped."

Except for a few old men, all the civilians had moved out because even the locals couldn't navigate through the neighborhoods. The roads were alive with IEDs—roadside bombs—and only the insurgents knew where they were. The Marines called the town Volcano City—even though the terrain was perfectly flat—because it was always erupting. The Americans did manage to dismantle quite a few of the bombs, but Karim kept putting in new ones. Every team of Marines that had gone in before Dan's had suffered casualties. Deaths. Blown-up legs. One team started out with seventeen men and ended with five. One of Dan's best friends, a kid named Tony, had marched into the village a cocky twenty-year-old and returned home a double amputee.

Dan and his men would move out at 2:30 in the morning. Since they had thermal optics and the insurgents didn't, the Marines could go in under cover of darkness and take their places before dawn. Sometime early in the morning, Karim would lay an IED in the only passable road in town—a sandy trail strewn with debris that Al-Qaida knew the Marines would have to travel. "Avenue of Death," the guys called it. Dan went over the aerial photographs showing countless scorched and flattened dwellings. Finally, he spotted a blown-out edifice that still had a roof. As staff sergeant, he would lead the squad of eleven men to the Avenue of Death and then to the abandoned building. Then they would wait for Karim.

Ironic, thought Dan. *Karim* meant "generous," "noble," "friendly," but this guy was the deadliest motherfucker in the pack. An expert IED-maker. An excellent shot. And ruthless. Rumor had it that he routinely gunned down children in front of their parents in order to coerce the fathers into cooperating with the rebels. First the youngest, and then, if Papa didn't go along with him, the next one... and so on. Dan couldn't wait to put a bullet between this guy's eyes.

He lit a cigarette and noticed with satisfaction that his hands weren't shaking. Karim would have backup, of course, but the Americans were all first-rate snipers. Dan had been winning prizes in marksmanship since he was a kid, and the others on the team were almost as good.

"Karim and his guys have it coming," Dan said to himself. "They're scum. They kill children. They plant bombs in schools and marketplaces. They deserve what we're gonna do to them." He inhaled deeply on his cigarette and caressed his rifle one last time. "They have it coming, don't they, sweetheart?" he said to his gun. "They really have it coming."

Dan had seen Karim, but he didn't know what the guy looked like. The terrorists wore black stockings over their heads to hide their faces. Dan closed his eyes an instant and imagined his nemesis. Penetrating eyes, black mustache, stubbly chin. Dan took another puff on his cigarette and imagined Karim planting the IED—maybe something as simple as a can with explosives and nails in it rigged up to a power supply such as a battery and detonated by a trip wire. Or maybe something more sophisticated than that. It didn't matter what it was, though, because Dan was going to bring him down before he laid his friggin' bomb.

In his mind's eye he could see the insurgent crouching in the street. He could feel his own blood pulsing, his muscles growing tense, his eyes focusing. He could smell his own sweat, slightly sweet, slightly acrid. He swallowed and steadied his breath. He felt himself pull the trigger. He imagined Karim's head exploding like a king-sized jar of salsa. Blood like tomato juice running into the gravel. Bam. Another shot. Muscle and flesh far and wide. Human hamburger. A feast. A veritable fucking feast… for a vulture.

"He's scum," Dan told the rifle. "Don't feel bad about it. We're the good guys."

By 2:30 a.m. they were in their trucks and pulling out. The men—all eleven of them— were wide awake, high on adrenaline. No one felt like talking. Dan stared at the moon hanging in the sky, white as a ghoul.

Dan thought about his mother. Iraq was seven hours ahead of the East Coast. Back home in Westlake Corner, it would be a bit after 7:30 in the evening. Mom would be washing up the dinner dishes, listening to the news on the radio, flinching every time the announcer mentioned Ramadi, or Mosul, or Baghdad. He had made sure that she never knew exactly where he was. He sent periodic emails:

"Everything is fine, Mom. Don't worry about a thing."

"But I just read that a car bomb went off in Ramadi! Were you there? Were you hurt?"

"No, Mom. It didn't go off anywhere near me! I'm actually nowhere near Ramadi." Dan hated lying to his mother. "Everything's pretty calm here where I am. No need to worry."

"Where are you?"

"Classified information, Mom. I can't tell you."

He called her right after they shipped Tony off to the medical center in Landstuhl to have his legs amputated. He kept his voice steady, but he could hear the strain in hers.

"Are you okay, Dan? I worry."

"I'm fine. Hey, the cookies you sent were delicious. Me and the guys loved them. You're the greatest, Mom!"

"But I just read…"

"Don't believe the newspapers, Mom. Those journalists don't have a rat's ass of an idea what's going on."

Sometimes he chatted with his sister, Kayla, by email.

"U no," wrote Kayla, "Mom's a mess. Doctor forbade her to read papers or watch the news."

"Sounds like she's doing it anyway."

"Westlake C News has nothing about I'q anyhow, but she watches TV and checks the Net all the time. She's obsessed. CNN, ABC, Fox. And every news web site U can imagine. All the time. It sucks."

"Hey, pig-face, you got a boyfriend yet?"

"Don't change the subject, Dan. How's your friend Tony?"

"He's fine. Listen, pig-face, gotta go. Watch over Mom. How's Dad, by the way?"

"He's killing himself w/ work. Puts in about 15 hours a day at the hardware store. Probably so he doesn't have to think too hard about what's going on with U. Doctor says his bl'd pressure is off the charts."

"Don't tell Mom."

"Of course not. But I'm trying to get him to lose weight. Hey, Dan, U miss Virginia? It's beautiful here in April. The forsythias r in bloom."

"Ain't nothing here in bloom, pig-face. Just sand and more sand, everywhere you look."

"Stay safe, Dan."

"Gotta go, Kayla."

"Bye, Dan."

"Bye, sweetheart. Take care of Mom."

Dan imagined his mother hanging up the dishtowel and sitting down at the kitchen table to grade homework papers. Her fourth-grade class would be just be starting long division now—26 into 832, 43 into 961. It's what kept her going—teaching arithmetic and spelling to twenty boisterous brats every year.

The moon's macabre pallor cast a muted beam on the metal of the truck. "Good a time as any to kill somebody," muttered Dan under his breath. He lit a cigarette and wondered if his mother had any idea that, at that very moment, he was on his way to take a man's life.

"My son's a Marine sniper in Iraq!" she told her friends proudly. Did she have any idea what that meant? Dan wondered.

And then another thought came to him: Karim had a mother too. What would she do when she found out her son was dead? Would she sob? Would she rend her clothes and tear her hair in the privacy of her home? Would she throw herself over his body at the public funeral? "Serves her right for raising a murderer," Dan said aloud to nobody.

They left the trucks about a mile from the town, well hidden behind some burned-out sheds, and walked the rest of the way.

"They've got it coming," muttered Bobby as he trudged along beside Dan. Bobby was a black-haired kid from South Dakota—part American Indian, maybe, or maybe something else.

"They certainly do," said Dan.

"The way they murder children right in front of their parents."

"It's unfathomable."

Twenty-three, stocky, fierce in battle, Bobby was, in Dan's opinion, a Marine's

Marine. "Bravest kid I know," was what Dan said about him.

"When God passes judgment on us all," whispered Bobby, "he's going to send Karim and all his ilk right to hell. I don't know what He'll do with me, but I'm sure He'll shove Karim into the express elevator down."

When they got to the Avenue of Death, the men moved into single file, and Bobby took his place at the head of the line. It was his job to test the road for explosives each step of the way so that the others could follow. Metal detector in hand, he checked a tiny swath, then stepped forward. The Marines followed. Then they repeated the procedure over and over again. Everyone knew that one missed spot could mean that Bobby or someone else would step on an explosive and be blown to pieces. Finally, Dan spotted the roofed building he had seen in the aerial photo. Half the men advanced gingerly into the structure and took their places. The other half took positions on the other side of the road.

As soon as the first group set foot inside the house, the metal detector went nuts.

"The whole place is booby-trapped," whispered Bobby.

"We've got to get to the roof," said Dan, "but without stepping on anything."

"We'll have to move slowly—but quickly," said Bobby. "I'll take each one up separately. It's the only way."

One by one, each Marine followed Bobby. Inch by inch, pace by pace, Bobby verified that the next step would be safe, standing on the spot in question himself, then signaling his buddies to advance. Dan told the radio operator to check in with the guys across the road and looked at his watch. It was 0515.

"He'll be by at any time," said Dan, his eyes fixed on the band of rubble and garbage that passed for a street in this godforsaken town.

By 10 a.m. there was still no sign of Karim.

"Y'all know what I want?" exclaimed Brian, a stocky, tough-looking, brown-haired guy from Alabama. "I want a large rib-eye steak, medium rare, three eggs, and some grits."

Dan chuckled. "Here," he said, throwing him an MRE, "eat this! Meal Ready to Eat. Between twelve hundred and five thousand calories. Official issue of the U.S. Military."

"Shit," mumbled Brian. "You know what MRE really stands for, don't ya? Meal Rejected by Everyone. I can't stand this crap anymore." He opened his package of spaghetti and meatballs, fished out the plastic spoon, and began to slurp.

"You know what I want?" chimed in Bobby. "I wanna get laid!"

"Fat chance!" teased Brian. "There ain't even a nanny goat around here. If there were, I'd fuck her myself!"

Dan wasn't hungry and he wasn't horny. He wasn't even tired. Every muscle in his body was tensed and ready for action. "Won't be long now, sweetheart," he whispered to his rifle.

He peered up and down the road. It was almost noon and the scorching sun was bearing down on the roof.

"Where the fuck is this guy?" muttered Bobby.

"Why? You got a date or something? Or maybe a board meeting? He'll be here any minute."

But of course, there was no telling when he'd be there.

By mid-afternoon he still hadn't appeared. Dan put down his rifle and crawled to a corner to urinate. "Don't blink," he whispered to the others. "Not even for a second."

At 1938—7:38 p.m.—one of the guys on the other side of the road hissed through the radio: "Where is this fucking bastard? It's dark already!"

"He'll be here."

"He probably won't come at night."

"Probably not. But you never know."

This is the worst part, thought Dan. The waiting. The tedium. Time seemed to travel at the pace of a drunken caterpillar. "He's playing mind games with us," said Dan to himself. "Usually he works in the morning, but today he's going to delay in order to throw us off. He's smart, this guy Karim. A real smart son of a bitch. But we're smarter. Whenever he gets here, we're going to send him right off to Jannah, that so-called Qu'ranic paradise where Allah will give him seventy-two virgins, white-skinned and bald beneath the eyebrows, and he can fuck all day long. Or maybe not. Maybe Bobby was right. More likely he'll go to Jahannam, the hell reserved for sons of bitches like him, baby-killers and torturers.

"Allah has no use for guys like you, I'm sure of it," Dan said to the absent Karim under his breath. "Allah doesn't want his followers mowing down innocents. Your Day of Judgment is coming, Karim, and Allah is going to send you directly to the deepest circle of hell."

It was almost dawn.

What if things turned out differently than anticipated? Dan thought suddenly. What if Karim and his men somehow popped out of nowhere and took them all down? "What if I shoot and miss, and then Karim turns my brains into guacamole?" he said to himself. "God, I don't want to check out in this godforsaken hole in the ground. Mom would die of grief. Dad might have a heart attack." Dan took a deep breath and hardened his jaw. "Stop it!" he said to himself. "You're falling right into Karim's trap. This is just what he wants. To debilitate us."

It wasn't until about 1045 the next morning that Bobby detected movement on the road. Dan squinted into the glare. He had been on watch for some thirty hours with just an occasional catnap, but he was alert and his senses were sharp.

Three figures came into view.

"Shit!" whispered Bobby.

"Hold your fire!" ordered Dan. He turned to the radio operator. "Tell the guys across the street to hold their fire."

"But Sargent Lesko!" countered Bobby. "We have our orders!"

"Don't shoot!" commanded Dan.

The three figures were more visible now—a man, a woman, and a little boy of about six or seven. Just like Karim to pay some desperate, starving family to do his dirty work, thought Dan.

"They're putting in an IED," said Bobby. "We have to take them out. That bomb could kill Americans."

Dan knew he had exactly three seconds to make a decision. He was a good enough shot to pick off the father and leave the woman and child unharmed.

"No. Hold your fire."

The family went to work putting in the bomb—a container, a plate—right in the middle of the narrow corridor. Inevitably, anyone using the road would step on it. They were remarkably efficient. Now they were covering it with dirt. In a moment they would be fleeing.

"Sergeant Lesko?"

"I'm not bringing down that guy in front of his kid, Bobby. I couldn't live with myself."

"But—"

"If we shoot that man, we'll have made an enemy for life. That little boy will never stop hating the Americans who killed his father and in ten years, I guarantee he'll be a terrorist. How'd you feel if someone mowed down your dad right in front of you?"

"Okay, you're right, Sergeant Lesko. But

Al-Qaida isn't so generous."

"That's the difference between them and us. Anyhow, if we kill that guy, Karim will just send in some other poor bastard to finish the job."

"Okay. I guess it's a judgment call."

"I couldn't sleep with a clear conscience if I took out a guy in front of his kid."

"What about Karim?"

"He's around here somewhere. He expected us to take out the family and then pick apart the bomb so he or one of his goons could blast us."

"Well, we've got to dismantle that fucking IED."

"I'm going to do it myself. You and the rest of the guys can cover me."

"With all due respect, Sergeant Lesko, that's crazy. Karim could be hiding anywhere. You can't expose yourself like that."

But Sergeant Lesko did expose himself, day after day, every time an Iraqi family with a child appeared to lay a roadside bomb on the Avenue of Death. Finally, his team was replaced with another. Lesko and his men piled into trucks in the middle of the night and headed back to base.

"Wish we would have got him," groused Bobby.

"Well, at least no Americans died on our watch," said Lesko. "And no kids, either."

* * *

Dan Lesko was back at Camp Pendleton, in California, when the e-mail came. It wasn't from anyone he knew. It was from someone in the platoon that had replaced his in Ramadi.

"Hi," it began. "We got Karim. He had a family lay a bomb and was waiting for us to come out so he could incinerate us. He was going to detonate the thing himself with a cell phone. The guys caught sight of him lurking behind a pile of rubble. We thought you'd want to know."

Dan laid his head in his hands and struggled not to weep for joy. He stroked his rifle a while and then he called Bobby.

"That's great," said Bobby. But he sounded let down. There was an awkward pause. "The thing is," he said finally, "I wish I could have got the motherfucker myself."

"Yeah," said Dan. "Me too. But it doesn't matter, Bobby. It really doesn't matter at all."

Interrogating Calla

Captain Brad Minden knew all the tricks. He knew what questions to ask, how to instill fear, how to catch people off guard. He knew how to apply pressure and how to "enhance" his techniques. At thirty-two, he was a crack interrogator, capable of squeezing information out of a rock. That was until they brought in Calla. Then everything went to hell.

The moment he laid eyes on her, a high-voltage surge jolted Minden to heightened awareness.

"Name?"

"Calla."

"Your complete name."

"That is my complete name."

"Are you married?"

"Iraqi women don't use their husbands' names. I'm sure you know that."

"I'm asking if you're married."

"No, I'm not married."

Minden felt his muscles relax. Why had that happened? He stared at the wall ahead, keeping his features impassive, his breath even. *It's because it's easier to question an unmarried woman,* he told himself, but he knew it wasn't true. It was because Calla was the most beautiful woman he had ever seen. Even more beautiful than his wife. He didn't want her to be married. He didn't want her to belong to someone else.

He shifted his gaze, glancing fleetingly at her face. It would be disrespectful to look at her directly, but still, he had to know: Had she noticed anything? Had he revealed emotion? "Approachable yet dispassionate," the trainer had told him years ago. No, apparently, he hadn't given anything away. All he saw in her eyes was fear, the fear of a doe who knows herself to be within rifle range of a hunter.

"Name?"

"Calla."

"What is your father's name?"

"Dawud al-Jamil."

"Are you the sister of Yahya?"

"No."

He thought she was lying. Yahya, the son of Dawud al-Jamil, had sent a donkey laden with explosives into a crowded marketplace the day before. Then he had detonated the load. The animal erupted into smithereens, spraying the vegetable stands with blood, guts, and bone and killing more than twenty sellers and shoppers. Or maybe he hadn't flipped the switch himself. Bystanders had seen a woman with him. She was wearing a black burka, covered from head to toe, but people said it was probably one of his sisters. Maybe Calla. Maybe Lana or Noora.

Of course, it could have been a brother disguised as a woman.

They'd picked up Calla in a side street, running away from the market. She was dressed the same as the woman whom onlookers had seen with Yahya—but so were all the other women in sight.

Minden considered his options. The technique he preferred, even with men, was not the one you read about in the newspapers. He knew how to stuff humus into a detainee's anus, of course, or to subject a prisoner to deafening noise. Twenty-four hours of Kraftwerk at 110 decibels could break just about any holdout. He understood the efficacy of punching, nakedness, and locking captives in coffins. But he knew—because he had read all the studies—that rapport building was the most effective approach to getting information. Detainees were fourteen times more likely to provide actionable intelligence when interrogators maintained a respectful or even a friendly demeanor and questioned them in a comfortable setting.

"Name?"

"Calla."

"Would you like a cup of tea?"

"What?"

"I thought it might help you relax."

Another glimpse at her eyes exposed the stupidity of the remark. He had terrified her. Her impossibly long lashes fluttered as she gaped at the folds of her *dishdasha*. "Relax!" That's probably what Al-Qaida prison guards said to their victims right before they raped them. Captain Minden pressed his lips together and composed his next sentence painstakingly, using his very clearest Arabic.

"I don't want to hurt you, Calla." He made his voice sound gentle. "I just need to find out a few things."

She lifted her hand and took the edge of her *hijab*, then wrapped it over the lower part of her face. Minden noticed that her hands were delicate and manicured, even though she wore no polish. They fluttered like tiny sparrows along the hem of her headscarf.

"Tell me about yourself, Calla. Do you work?"

Calla stared down at her knees.

"Some interrogators are rough, Calla. I don't want to be rough. I just want to ask you a few questions. Answer them, and you'll be that much closer to getting out of here."

"I was a teacher," she whispered. "Before the Americans."

"What kind of teacher?"

"Little girls."

"That's lovely. Did you have a favorite pupil?"

Calla glowered at the table that separated them. She shrugged, as if to convey that the question was so nonsensical that she wouldn't deign to answer it.

"My sister is a teacher," said Minden. "She teaches second grade. She loves it."

Calla remained motionless.

Minden signaled the female guard to take her back to the cell. "I think she's had enough," he said. "I'll have another go at it tomorrow."

That afternoon Brad Minden collapsed on his cot and fell into a deep sleep. It was his first break in about thirty hours. He dreamed about Calla, her gilt-colored irises, her elongated, almond-shaped eyes, her fringe-like lashes, her sculptured cheeks, her flawless skin, as smooth and golden as honey. In his dream she was smiling at him, her amber-rose lips parted slightly, her cheeks flushed. She raised one sparrow-like hand and rested it coquettishly on her chin. In his dream, he saw himself push her scarf back over a dainty ear.

A door slammed. Minden lurched forward on his cot and opened his eyes. On a clumsy wooden table that served as a nightstand, Katherine—blond, blue-eyed, and plump—and their two daughters smiled out at him from a framed photo. Minden pressed the photo to his lips, then bent over to lace up his boots. He felt like crap. It was Katherine, not his sister, who was a second-grade teacher. He was being dishonest with everybody.

* * *

Brad Minden had interrogated Calla eight times over the past two weeks, and he thought that he was finally getting somewhere.

"Tell me something about your family," he coaxed.

"I have three sisters," she said, finally. "Lala, Noora, and the baby, Sara."

"How old is Sara?"

"Seven." Minden thought he saw a smile flicker across Calla's lips when she mentioned Sara.

He smiled at her. "I see you love little Sara very much," he said gently. "Do you have any brothers?"

Calla's jaw tightened. She shrugged her shoulders to show she had no intention of answering.

"Do you recognize this man?" He showed her an intel photograph of Yahya—heavy eyebrows and beard, but the same gilt-touched, almond-shaped eyes as Calla.

Calla stared at the photo, expressionless.

"Do you like American movies?" asked Minden, changing the subject abruptly. It was a tactic he'd learned to throw the detainee off guard.

"I've never seen a movie."

"What about American music? You like Mariah Carey?"

Calla's face lit up. "'We Belong Together'!" She started singing softly in broken English. "'Come back, baby. Please come…'"

Minden chimed in. "'Come back, baby. Please come back.' What other music do you like? Anything I might know?"

"'Shake it Off'!" She was smiling now. "We can get pirated copies."

"Another Mariah Carey! I like that one, too."

"But she's not a very nice girl."

"Mariah Carey? What do you mean? Why not?"

"The way she dresses. She's immodest."

Minden smiled. "It's that... women dress differently in the States. Customs are... well, not like here."

"It's disgusting!"

"Yes, well, maybe."

Suddenly Calla bit her lip and turned away from him.

"Are you tired, Calla? Shall we call it quits for today?" He signaled to the female guard, who took Calla by the arm and escorted her out.

* * *

Three weeks had passed since their first interview, and Minden had learned almost nothing of importance.

"It takes time," he told his commanding officer. "Sometimes weeks. Sometimes months. You have to be patient."

But Major Henderson was growing exasperated. "Yahya al-Jamil blew up a mosque the other day. We're sure it was him. The donkey. The explosives. Same MO as before. Then he disappears into thin air."

"Have you brought in the sisters?"

"The neighbors think they're in Syria. But Yahya is here, and we've got to nab him before he blows up something else."

As the guard brought in Calla, Minden

struggled not to notice the way the white *dishdasha* flowed and fluttered over her body. She moved like a dancer, with graceful, even steps that propelled her so lightly that she seemed to skim the floor.

"Name?"

"You know my name," she whispered. She looked up at him with her enormous hazel eyes tinged with gold.

"I like to hear you say it," he said softly. "It's a beautiful name."

She's falling in love with me, thought Minden. *She'll tell me anything I want to know. I just have to bide my time.*

Suddenly Minden felt as though a wad of pitch were coagulating in his stomach. *This is wrong,* he told himself. *I can't take advantage of this girl. She cares for me. I can't use her feelings against her. It's just... I don't know... depraved.*

"Are you married?" Calla asked abruptly.

Minden looked up, startled.

"Why do you ask?"

"It's normal for a man your age to be married."

Minden thought a moment about what he should say. If he said no, she would think him strange. An Iraqi man in his early thirties would be married. But if he said yes, she would think he'd been leading her on. She'd turn against him and clam up. Minden jerked back to reality. He had a job to do. She was opening up, and it didn't matter whether it was because she loved him—falling for your captor, the famous Stockholm syndrome he'd learned about—or because he'd finally worn her down. He had to proceed carefully.

"Yes," he said simply. "I'm married."

He searched her face for disappointment, bitterness, anger. Instead, he saw her features soften.

She turned to him and smiled. This time it wasn't a simper or a smirk, but a real smile.

"Yahya isn't my brother," she whispered. "He's my cousin. And I wasn't with him that day. It was Noora."

It occurred to him that she might be lying.

"Where is Noora now?" he asked.

"They've all left the country. If I ever get out of here, I'll follow them. We have relatives in Al-Qaim, on the border. They will take me to Ar-Raqqah, where my mother and sisters are waiting. I hate this place... all this bombing, all this killing. Noora, she's a fighter. She loves the excitement of war. But not me."

"Where is Yahya?"

"I don't know, but I'm guessing he'll strike again, maybe in the market. His favorite day is Thursday because people are getting ready for the Sabbath."

Minden filed his report and recommended that Calla be released. He felt guilty about the interrogation. He had manipulated her emotions—an unmanly tactic, although better than locking her in a dark cell crawling with lizards. Now it was his duty to get her out of prison.

* * *

A few weeks later, Minden was navigating through a narrow, winding street toward the market when he caught sight of a familiar face. A woman in a black burka. Only her eyes were visible, but Minden was certain he wasn't mistaken. The honey-hued slivers of visible skin, the enormous, almond-shaped eyes, lids fringed in black silk, gold-specked irises. She looked up and caught his gaze. He couldn't see her mouth, but he was sure she was smiling.

Suddenly, she raised her hand as if to signal someone.

Minden turned. Yahya appeared in a doorway. He looked right at the American and smiled. Then he stuck his hand into the folds of his *dishdasha*.

By the time Captain Minden saw the revolver, it was too late.

A Good Old American Breakfast

Jamali didn't want to work with the Americans, but he needed the money. He had plenty of reasons to detest the foreigners. His sixteen-year-old cousin Zaid had been caught in the crossfire at an American checkpoint and lost an arm, and Jamali had lost his livelihood because now nobody bought the fine wooden cabinets he made. Americans had brought war to Iraq, and war had left the country in shambles. Jamali thought about it a long time before he accepted the offer from Lt. Montez.

"You have to be practical," Jamali said, sighing.

His cabinetry shop, where he and Zaid worked together, lay practically dormant. With Marines kicking in doors and bombs going off all over the place, no one ventured out, either to work or to buy. Jamali sat in his shop with his saws and lathes, his bits and sanders, and waited. No one came because no one had money. Besides, how could you think about fancy breakfronts with graceful curlicues and arabesques when you knew your house could be rubble in the morning?

"The Americans will pay fifty dollars for information about a weapons cache," Jamali told his wife, Amira, "and a hundred for information about an Al-Qaida operative. More, if the guy is important. American money, not dinars. Zaid thinks I have to do it."

"It's dangerous," said Amira. "If you get caught, Al-Qaida will kill you."

Jamali looked around the shop. His handiwork filled the place. Ornate dressers with drawers exquisitely carved in intricate floral designs. Picture frames with trompe d'oeil geometric patterns. Tall, sturdy wall cabinets trimmed with wooden spirals that reminded you of the whirling vortices of a sandstorm. Jamali was a master craftsman, as his father and grandfather had been before him and his cousin was becoming before he'd lost his arm. But what good was such skill and talent if you couldn't put food on the table? Amira couldn't stew and season fine furniture for dinner.

Jamali's three sons—Abrahem, Gaban, and Gabir, age seven to twelve—spent the day in the workshop learning to whittle and carve or sweeping up sawdust. His eight-year-old daughter Aasera sewed by her mother's side. The madrassas were closed. Even if they had been open, no reasonable father would send his children to school. The streets were too dangerous.

"We are decaying here," Jamali told Amira. "What will the children eat if I can't sell anything?"

"But informing for the Americans..." She looked down at her hands and pursed her lips. "Look where that got Hakim the baker."

Jamali stifled a moan that sounded more like a sob. Hakim had collected enough money from the Marines to buy a new oven. One morning he opened his front door to find the body of his oldest son bleeding into the gravel of the front path, his hands tied behind his back and his throat slit. Hakim's screams brought Jamali and the other neighbors running. That afternoon, they heard one final gut-slashing cry. Hakim had thrown himself into the oven.

"I don't know what to do," whispered Jamali.

"You scout and I'll give them the information," said Zaid. "That way, if Al-Qaida takes vengeance on anybody, it will be on me."

"I can't do that," said Jamali.

"I have no wife and children," countered Zaid, "and now I can't work. I'm no good to anyone. I might as well do what I can to help."

"They say Montez pays fast. He checks out the tip, and if it's good, he hands over the cash right away. Very businesslike. Very dependable."

* * *

I was glad to hear it. Ignacio Montez is my son, and I'd heard he was respected not only by the Marines, but also by the Iraqis. Not that he ever told me much about what he experienced over there, but the men he served with sometimes take me aside at events for military families and tell me stories. Some even send me emails. Once Ignacio invited a bunch of Marines over for breakfast, and I caught snippets of their conversation while I was in the kitchen. They were talking about Jamali and Amira.

"It was so awful when Zaid lost his arm," someone said. "I hate when something like that happens at a checkpoint."

Then I guess Ignacio realized I was eavesdropping and hushed them up.

"We haven't had a breakfast this good since that time back when…"

Suddenly the room was quiet. Then, after a pause, they started talking about football.

I spend long hours imagining the stories people tell me about Ignacio, replaying them in my mind over and over like beloved videos, first changing this detail, then changing that. I envisage Jamali in a *dishdasha*, the ankle-length robe I've seen on men in pictures, white or maybe cream, a red-checkered *kaffiyeh* on his head. I imagine his stone-gray eyes squinting at the hem of the sky, his jaw tensed in pain. I imagine him in his workshop, sanding rough wood into a smooth surface, the morning's work on his sandaled feet. He is wondering if anyone will buy the pretty little chest he is making just to keep busy. I hear the groans in his anguished heart. I visualize Zaid, his arm like the stump of a branch hit by lightning. Skin like sandpaper. Mustache like a black-bristled toothbrush. A gaze as intense and piercing as an eagle's. And Amira. What does she look like? A spindle-shaped specter in a flowing *dishdasha* made of cotton, but silky-looking in the sunlight that filters through the pane. She wears a *hijab* like a vaporous aura over her hair. A phantom of a woman trapped between the terror of starvation and the savagery of war. A woman exhausted by anxiety and sleeplessness, just like me. Two mothers, Amira and I, worlds apart, but caught in the same nightmare. She fears for her children, as I fear for my son. The difference is, for her, the violence is in her yard. For me, it's in my head.

Ignacio had met Jamali one day when he kicked in his door. The Marines had heard that there were Al-Qaida hiding in the area, and they were searching all the houses. Surprisingly—to me, but not to the young Marine who told me the story the first time I heard it—Jamali asked Ignacio and his men to stay for tea.

"Tea?" I said. "But you'd just kicked in his door!"

"That's the way they are, ma'am," he said. "Once you're in their house, you're their guest."

Jamali assured the Marines that he wasn't interested in politics. He didn't like Al-Qaida, but he didn't like foreigners occupying his country, either. So no, he told Ignacio, when my son first broached the subject, he wouldn't help the Americans.

But things had changed. The money situation was dire. Jamali had to find a way to feed his family.

"All right," Jamali told Ignacio, "but just for a little while. Just until I get back on my feet."

By then, Ignacio had drunk tea with Jamali many times. He had seen his workshop and met his family. He had even given him a few small gifts of meat and cheese. Ignacio thanked Jamali in Arabic—he'd made it his business to learn a bit of the language—and told him he'd be back.

"It will look like a regular patrol," said Ignacio. "I'll kick in the door so no one will suspect you of collaborating."

Jamali and Zaid kept their eyes open. Within days, they had tips for Ignacio. An IED planted during the night. A weapons cache hidden under a school building. Jamali could once again buy essentials for his family, but Amira stirred the lamb and barley stew with a nervous hand.

"I'm only doing it for the money," Jamali told her. "It's a short-term arrangement."

Amira didn't believe him. She could tell that her husband was beginning to like the Americans—or perhaps, he was just growing more disgusted with Al-Qaida. The insurgents were becoming more vicious. They called themselves Sunnis but, Jamali told his wife, their barbarous acts had nothing to do with Sunnism. Look at what they had done to Ali, the rich businessman who had investments in England and a large house with two wives. Ali was a self-confident man, used to speaking his mind. Once, at a town meeting, he'd protested the way the insurgents used women and children as shields when the Americans attacked their enclaves. The next day, neighbors found Ali's naked and tortured body tied to a post by the road. It was headless.

"These people are repulsive," Jamali told Amira. "They are worse than animals."

"Stay out of it," she said.

She'd noticed that Jamali was pursuing information to give to Ignacio Montez with increased energy.

"The American lieutenant won't save you if you fall into the wrong hands," said Amira. "And Allah forbid that they get any of the children." She burst into tears. I'd burst into tears, too. That's what any mother would do.

Jamali was passing actionable information on to Ignacio nearly every day now. A bomb planted in the souk. Explosives under the mosque. A high-value target in an abandoned house. Ignacio either dealt with it or passed it on to his commander, Col. Chang, who got the Marines any additional men or material they might need to deal with the situation. Thanks to Jamali, Ignacio and his men were able to make real progress cleaning up the precinct. Chang was delighted. The Marines were delighted. Jamali breathed more easily now that he had an income. Only

Amira still floated through the house like a spirit, her face turning ever paler with every new bag of rice or wheat that Jamali brought into the one large all-purpose room in which the family lived. She'd taken to keeping the children within view at all times. She didn't even let the boys go into the shop with Jamali, although it was right next door and attached to the house. No playing in the street. No soccer. You couldn't take a chance. As for Aasera, she sat by her mother sewing, just as she had since they closed the schools.

Jamali still had no customers, but every once in a while, neighbors saw him carrying a hen or leading a bleating, tethered lamb down the street. Perhaps someone reported him, or perhaps one of the goons spotted him. It's clear that someone suspected something.

One day, as Abrahem stood by a window pouring water from a jug, a murky shadow appeared on the wall. Amira shrieked. The other children rushed into Jamali's shop. Just as Jamali passed through the passage between his workspace and the family's living quarters, three hooded men pushed through the door and grabbed the child. A black-clad arm pressed against his throat. Then two black-gloved hands popped a sack over his head and yanked him through the door.

"Say good-bye to your baby," snarled the intruder.

Paralyzed, Amira saw her youngest son disappear, as though in a hallucination. Her legs were suddenly stumps. Her eyes were bulging like a toad's. Then, suddenly, she erupted like a mortar round, howls and screams piercing the air.

"I told you!" she shrieked. "I'd rather eat wood than *this*! Allah! Allah! Anything but this!"

I imagine her cries, like sirens wailing through the city. I feel her agony in my own gut. My own body quavers and quakes. What can she do? What would I do?

Jamali took off for the base to get Ignacio, but the Marines already knew what had happened.

"I need the best intel available on where those bastards are hiding the kid," screamed Ignacio into the radio. Chang was barking data to bases in surrounding areas.

"They won't take him far," he said grimly. "Not if they want to kill him and make a spectacle of it in order to set Jamali up as an example. If that's their plan, and it probably is, they'll do it tomorrow, in broad daylight. That gives us less than twenty-four hours to find the kid."

By nightfall Ignacio had information about where Abrahem might be—six or eight possibilities, a lot of territory to cover in one night. He divided a portion of his platoon into four teams. The teams would check out the leads, while the remainder carried out their regular duties.

One spot on Ignacio's list was an abandoned mechanic's shop just out of town. It had been empty for a while, and sand had piled up along the side of the building, partially blocking it from view. A guard was leaning against the front door, smoking a cigarette. Just one, which was unusual. Undoubtedly, there would be other men inside.

The Marines snuck around the side of the building and hid behind the chassis of a rust-eaten vehicle. Ignacio waited for the right moment, then, in a single stride, moved behind the guard and stuffed his fist into the man's mouth while pinning his arms behind his back.

"Don't speak, just nod," whispered Ignacio.

The man tried to bite Ignacio's hand, but then spotted three other Marines, their pistols trained at his forehead.

"Are there other guys in the house?"

The guard nodded no, but Ignacio assumed he was lying.

"Is Jamali the cabinetmaker's son in there?"

"No."

"Do you know where he is?"

The man hesitated a moment. He seemed overcome with indecision. He was young, maybe eighteen, still almost beardless, perhaps not yet a hardened rebel. Finally, he nodded yes. His head barely moved.

"Radio for backup," Ignacio told one of the men. "We don't know what we'll find inside." Then he turned to the guard: "Where's the boy?"

Ignacio lowered his hand slightly so that the guard could answer.

"If you want to live," snapped Ignacio, "show us where the kid is."

The guard led Ignacio and two others to a small, dim room attached to the back of the mechanic's shop. Ignacio found Abrahem with his hands tied, whimpering, and sprawled out in a pool of his own urine, but alive.

One of the other Marines handcuffed the guard to take back to the base. The rest searched the shop and, to their surprise, found it empty. Ignacio picked the boy up and carried him back to the Humvee.

Ignacio climbed into the passenger seat and threw a blanket over his knees. Then he lifted in the sticky, smelly child.

"Are you okay?" Ignacio whispered.

Abrahem was too dazed to answer. He continued to whimper softly, until finally he dozed off on Ignacio's lap.

Back at the base, Ignacio stuck Abrahem under the shower and made him wash his body and his hair. The boy squealed as the water trickled down his back, over his head, into his eyes, but he allowed Ignacio to dry him with a towel and slip a Marine T-shirt over his tiny, seven-year-old body. Then he ate two MREs, while Ignacio did the paperwork. Ignacio would have liked to send him home with a clean set of clothes, but the souk had been closed for months because of the violence, so he washed out Abrahem's shorts and shirt and let them dry in the hot sun while the boy slept.

Ignacio hid Abrahem in a large sack, which he slung over his back. Then he went to Jamali's house and kicked in the door, now so splintered at the edges from frequent boot blows that it would soon have to be replaced.

Jamali and Amira stood there staring at the Marine, certain that he brought grim news.

Then Ignacio opened the sack and handed the boy to his mother. For a moment, Amira stood speechless. Then she began to rock back and forth as though she were going to faint. She gasped for breath and held her hands against her temples, blinking hard. She must have thought the image before her was an illusion. Suddenly, she let out a squeal and began to sob, only this time, they were sobs of joy. Finally, she regained her bearings. She ran her fingers through Abrahem's hair, touched his cheek, lifted his face toward hers.

"*Allahu Akbar!*" she said softly.

"My friend," whispered Jamali to Ignacio, kissing him on both cheeks. "Thank you. *Shukran jazīlan.* Please come to the house tomorrow morning with those who helped you so I can show my appreciation. And," he added, "enter the usual way."

One day at breakfast, months after Ignacio had returned from Iraq, I mentioned the incident to him. It was the only time we ever spoke of it.

"Oh, that," he said. "All in a day's work, Mom. But you should have heard Amira bawl when she had her kid back."

"Well, I should think so. And what was that business about a breakfast?"

"Huh? What breakfast?"

"Once when your friends were over, they said something…"

"Ah! You *were* snooping!"

"No, no… not really."

"Well, the day after we brought Abrahem home, we went over to Jamali's and kicked in the door as usual. To our amazement, Amira had laid out the most amazing American breakfast for us—like nothing I'd ever seen over there. Eggs and toast, cereal and yoghurt, coffee, juice. No bacon, of course—Muslims don't eat pork—but everything else you could imagine. Pancakes, syrup. I have no idea where they got that stuff! They were such kind people. They wanted so much to show their gratitude."

I imagine Jamali, Zaid, and the Marines sitting on the floor, steaming cups of American coffee before them. I imagine Amira laying out all that food and then disappearing into another part of the house. Yes, I know it's unfair that, as a woman, she wasn't allowed to take part in the celebration, but the most important thing is that she got her little boy back, and for that I am profoundly glad.

"Around then, Col. Chang was getting ready to redeploy back to the States," Ignacio went on. "The men really loved him, and they wanted to give him a nice present. I asked

Jamali if he could make a plaque for us with the Marine Corps emblem—you know, the Eagle, Globe, and Anchor. I gave him a picture to copy."

"Did he do it?"

"Mom, you wouldn't believe the magnificent wall-hanging he made for us—a huge circular panel of fine wood, with the most intricate carving. A perfect eagle, with every feather, every claw in place. A globe with all the continents. He wouldn't take any money for it! We tried to pay him, but he said, no, it was a gift."

"What happened to them? Do you know?"

"Well, right after that, the Sunni Awakening started. All the Sunnis started helping the Marines, and so then it wasn't so dangerous. Jamali and his cousin became regular collaborators, and that allowed us to bring Al-Qaida under control. By the time I returned to Iraq the second time, the area was so peaceful we could spend our time rebuilding."

This is the story I want to replay in my mind—the rare and beautiful story with a happy ending. I don't want to think about ISIS and what they do to people who helped our soldiers, like Jamali. I don't want to think about where Jamali and his family are now, or to ask myself if we are responsible.

Captain O'Reilly and the Professor

"The burns only covered her right arm and side. It could have been worse. Normally we would perform an escharotomy, but under the circumstances…"

"What's an escharotomy?"

"It's a surgical procedure you have to do when both the epidermis and the dermis are destroyed. You have to cut through the damaged skin down to the subcutaneous fat and into the healthy area. She was so tiny that the doctor didn't want to do it, but there was no other way to save the tissue. I prepared the dressings for the wound."

"What about the mother?"

"Dead. The explosion had blown both of them about ten yards, maybe more, but somehow the woman had managed to hold onto her baby and even shield the little body with her own. The guys said the mother was still alive when they pulled her out of the rubble, but by the time they got her to us, she was gone. She was lying there on a sheet, her head cocked in an awkward position, like a chicken with a broken neck. Half her body was incinerated—a mass of gory, buff- and wine-colored wounds that reminded me of a smashed plum. The baby was lying next to her, screaming. I picked the little thing up as gently as I could and held her a moment, but there was no time for sentiment. I handed her over to the docs. They worked like demons to keep blood flowing into the damaged area. Professor Thurston should have been there, the son of a bitch."

I smiled. "Yes, he should have been there," I said. "What happened to the little girl?"

"The woman had no identification on her, but eventually an uncle came looking for a missing niece and claimed the body. He took the child. He was sobbing. This was the second niece he had lost to Al-Qaida grenades and the second child he was going to have to raise on his own. I saw one of the aides hand him a few dinars. 'The U.S. government will send you a check,' he whispered through an interpreter, 'but who knows how long that will take.' The man pushed the money away. 'Please,' said the soldier. 'To buy medicine for the little girl.' He turned away to hide his tears from the man and also from me. 'You're not supposed to do that, Private Hansen,' I whispered. 'I don't give a shit,' he answered, and we left it at that.

* * *

I had never had a boarder like Captain O'Reilly. As slight as a feather and as black as a raven in an oil slick, she exuded strength — not physical strength, although she was wiry and tough, but inner strength. I liked her steady gaze and get-to-work-or-get-out-of-my-way attitude. She was a woman who meant business.

"Guess I wasn't what you expected," she said when she first stepped into my living room. Her application read: Captain C.W. O'Reilly, U.S. Army. "You were probably expecting a tall, broad-shouldered, blond guy, and here I'm a petite black woman. I'll be a good tenant, though. I pay my bills on time."

"That's fine, Captain O'Reilly. I need your full name for my records."

"Sandra Winifred O'Reilly. My great-great-grandfather was probably a slave on some Irishman's plantation." She said it matter-of-factly, without bitterness. "You can call me Sandra," she said, "but please, not Sandy."

I had never rented to a woman before. I was delighted. I thought she might be a companion for me. Although most of the time

Sandra was in class or in her room studying, occasionally, late at night, she'd come to the kitchen, and we'd share a pot of tea. She'd tell me stories, like the one about the little girl with the burns, or she'd describe her latest run-in with Professor Thurston.

"I went into the Army right out of high school," she explained, "and got shipped off to Iraq as a combat medic—a 68W, or Whisky. The Whiskies were the guys who provided emergency medical care for wounded soldiers, but sometimes they'd bring in an Iraqi civilian too. The docs all said I was a demon worker and had the brains to be a doctor myself. After a couple of years, I decided to go back to school and get a B.A. The Army was willing to help. I completed the degree in three years, became a second lieutenant, and applied to medical school."

Now she was a captain and a second-year medical student at the local university. Her courses in molecular and cellular biology, general chemistry, and neurobiology were going fine, she assured me. The thorn in her side was a required seminar she called a "touchy-feely shit course": The Physician and Society, taught by Dr. Donald Thurston, a renowned pacifist.

He began his first lecture with Latin

words he knew no one would understand: *Victus quoque rationem ad aegrotantium salutem pro facultate, judicioque meo adhibebo, noxamvero et maleficium propulsabo.* "He stared at me when he said them," Sandra chuckled. "And then, as though he were Jesus preaching the Sermon on the Mount, he thundered, 'These words are part of the Hippocratic Oath. *Do no harm.'* I knew he was trying to pick a fight with me. There were fifteen people in the room, but he was glaring right at me."

"Well, you have to get through the course," I told her, "so I guess you'll have to grin and bear it."

"Then he went on, 'The word *ahimsa,* to do no harm, is the core of pacifistic Buddhism and Hinduism. So, you see, a physician must be a pacifist. One cannot be both a soldier and a doctor. The concepts are diametrically opposed.'"

"'With all due respect, sir,' I said, 'soldiers do not declare war; governments do. And when a nation sends its military men and women into battle, some will be wounded. Doctors must attend to them.'"

"'Don't call me sir,' he snapped. 'This isn't an Army base!' The mole on his nose was trembling like a beetle in the rain. He turned away from me and started talking about Aung

San Suu Kyi, the Buddhist nonviolent, pro-democracy activist in Myanmar."

I hardly saw Sandra for the next couple of days. She got home late from the library or the lab. She was studying hard, trying to learn all she could. She was anxious to validate the Army's faith in her and also to avoid irritating Thurston.

"You know, it wasn't all burns and bullet wounds," she told me one evening while we were sipping wine. "Sometimes it's some tiny little thing you can do for a fellow soldier that makes your life worthwhile."

She closed her eyes, remembering.

"We were on this remote base with a makeshift medical facility—just an unenclosed space in the corner of the building. Iraq is hard on women. The sand is so fine-grained and powdery, it gets into all the wrong places. One of the sergeants had an infection, and she'd gone to see the doctor, who told her he had more urgent things to attend to. She insisted, so he had her lie down on a table, naked below the waist, knees splayed. Then he hiked up to her neck the sheet she had draped over herself. Soldiers were coming in and out. Most were sensitive enough to look away, but I could tell from this woman's face that she was mortified."

"Did you say something?"

"I just walked over and lowered the sheet, arranging it over her knees. The doctor could still perform his examination but without exposing her to the entire company. If you could have seen the look of relief and gratitude in that sister's eyes!"

I sighed and shook my head, then poured us both another glass of wine.

"How's it going with Thurston?" I asked cautiously.

"That guy's got a head full of rotting fish. The worst thing anyone could wish on him would be to be himself. You know what he said to me today? He said, 'What'd you do when they brought in an Iraqi civilian? Feed him cyanide pills?' I didn't answer him. I just walked away. Last week he asked me how many babies I'd killed over there. He's obsessed with dead babies. He never asks how many children's lives I've saved! Then he asked me if I got a recommendation to medical school by sleeping with my commanding officer. I thought men could be insensitive in the Army, but I've never met anyone as insensitive as this civilian pacifist."

"You ought to complain to someone. There must be some kind of a grievance office on campus."

"I can handle it alone. The last thing I need is for the Army to hear that I got into a fight with my professor."

But the situation kept getting worse. Thurston had assigned an essay on the physician's social responsibility to protect the public from threats of nuclear proliferation, climate change, environmental toxins, or violence caused by economic inequity. Sandra wrote about emergency care for victims of gun violence in urban hospitals.

"That wasn't the topic!" he barked at her in front of the whole class.

"Savagery in the streets is often due to poverty and despair, sir. Young men can't get jobs, so they turn away from society and engage in destructive—and self-destructive— behavior."

"Or they go into the Army where they can kill with impunity and win medals for it. And don't call me sir!"

Sandra bit her lip and stared straight ahead at the screen of her laptop.

A few weeks went by without her mentioning Thurston. I served dinner to the boarders every night at 7:00, but Sandra rarely joined us, preferring to grab a sandwich after her last lab and head directly for the library. When she returned after midnight, I was usually in bed. After a while, it occurred to me that she might be avoiding me. Maybe I was asking too many questions, I thought. Maybe she didn't want to talk about the Army, about classes, about Thurston.

But one Saturday evening, when the other boarders were out on dates or drinking at some bar with their buddies, she suggested we go out to a movie. We checked the newspapers but couldn't find a film that interested us, so we finally decided to stay home and watch *The Hurt Locker* on television.

I watched the roadside bombs go off, producing mile-high explosions, and grimaced.

"It wasn't like that at all," she grumbled when it was over.

"You mean the guys who get an adrenaline high dismantling bombs?"

"In my experience, all the bomb squad wants to do is deactivate the thing and get the hell out of there. They don't get a big thrill out of risking their lives every day pulling apart explosives." She paused and thought about it a minute. "When they're injured, you know what the first thing they ask is?"

"Whether you notified their mothers?"

She burst out laughing. "No! They ask whether they've still got their balls! They don't care whether they've lost a leg or an eye, as long as their manhood is intact."

"I can understand that," I said, thinking about my own son.

"You know," she said, changing the subject, "once a young girl came to me, a military policewoman. She'd gotten pregnant by one of the guys and miscarried the baby. Her uniform pants were soaked with blood, and she didn't know what to do. She was terrified her commanding officer would find out."

"You had to report it, didn't you?"

"What for? It was too late to save the baby. I performed a D&C, bandaged her up and put her to bed. I told the lieutenant in charge that she had a shrapnel wound, a superficial one that was expected to heal quickly, but that she should stay in the infirmary for a couple of days. I kept an eye on her until she was able to shoulder a rifle. No one ever found out about it."

"If you had it to do over again, would you join?"

"Of course. A handful of pigs and jerks wear the uniform, but most of the guys are terrific. I love the Army! I was just a poor kid from a carcass of a neighborhood in Chicago. I lived on a street that smelled of shit and cheap marijuana. The Army gave me confidence and taught me skills. My commanders were supportive, encouraging. It's thanks to them that I'm in medical school. How else could someone like me get to where I am now?" Suddenly her voice went quivery. "I thought that someday I'd go back and open a clinic in my old community. God knows those folks need one. But now it looks like I might not get through."

"What do you mean?"

"Professor Thurston made it pretty clear that he wasn't going to let me pass. He stood in front of the whole class and spat out syllables as though they were bullets. He said he had no intention of educating murderers and agents of destruction so that they could go back and wreak more havoc. 'We wouldn't need Army medics,' he hissed, 'if it weren't for these fucking wars!' 'No one hates war more than a soldier who's been through one, *sir!*' I hissed back. 'But as long as we have them, we need military doctors, and I intend to become one!' Some of the other students snickered and some just looked away."

"Sandra!" I felt as though I had a wad of cobwebs in my throat. "You have to go see the dean. You've worked so hard… you can't let this man—"

"He doesn't seem to realize that scores of Iraqi civilians came to us begging for help. Al-Qaida was kidnapping their children to use as human shields and raping little girls in order to intimidate their fathers into submission. War wreaks havoc, there's no denying it, but my job wasn't to kill. It was to save as many people as I could."

"Listen, Sandra, if Dr. Thurston wants to be a pacifist, that's his business. He has a constitutional right to his opinions. But he has no right to impose those opinions on his students, and he certainly has no right to humiliate you in public... or in private, for that matter!"

"I just don't want... problems." Suddenly tears like slivers of glass flooded her cheeks.

How can this be? I thought. How has this monster brought a strong, beautiful, principled young woman to tears? I never thought I'd see Sandra O'Reilly cry, but this brutish professor, with absolutely no understanding of the true meaning of *ahimsa*, was crushing her.

I handed her a Kleenex, then took her hand and squeezed it. "Go to see him in his office," I coaxed. "Up in front of the class, he has to play the tough, uncompromising idealist. After all, he has a reputation to uphold. But sometimes, even a brute will soften when you talk to him one-on-one. Don't be confrontational. Explain that you're an idealist, too. You want to save your neighborhood, just as he wants to save the world." I gave her another hanky. "Frankly, if I had to bet on one of you reaching your goal, I'd bet on you."

She shook her head. "It won't do any good," she whispered. "He won't listen."

Nevertheless, a week or so later, she pulled her jacket over her ears and pushed out into the icy, razor-sharp wind toward the Salk Building, where Thurston had his office. It was one of those days that turn your lips and nose brittle, and you feel like you have hoarfrost in your throat. But she had to do *something*, she told me. The situation had deteriorated. Thurston was ignoring her in class, not recognizing her when she raised her hand, not answering her questions.

She didn't ask for permission. She just walked in and sat down. He looked smaller up close than in the classroom, she said. His face was white as milkstone, as chiseled as a statue. "A prim, starched little man," was how she described him. The mole on his nose had taken on a reddish hue. It reminded her of a ladybug that wanted to take off on its own.

She had prepared a speech. She was going to explain her desire to use her medical knowledge to transform her neighborhood and why passing this course was so important to her. Instead, she sat there in silence, her eyes darting around the room.

The books on the shelves were predictable: *The Power of Non-Violence, Pacifism through the Ages, Christian Pacifism and Just War Theory.* She noticed a rather large section on Vietnam. *A First-Hand Account of the Vietnam War, A Bright Shining Lie,* Tim O'Brien's *The Things They Carried,* and four or five rows of volumes on the My Lai massacre, that fatal encounter in which U.S. Army officers killed some 500 unarmed Vietnamese civilians, including women, children, and babies, in 1968.

Sandra wanted to say something. Terrible things happened in war, she wanted to tell him. People went mad with grief and rage and lost control of themselves. They became brutes. It had happened at Abu Ghraib. It had happened in Haditha. But that didn't mean that all soldiers… The words turned leaden in her throat.

She noticed a photograph on one of the shelves—a young man, perhaps twenty-five or twenty-eight, seated on a rock. He wore shorts and a T-shirt. His feet were bare. His lips were pulled back in an easy grin. He bore a definite resemblance to Thurston, but he was better looking and seemed more relaxed.

"Your son?" she said finally.

She knew it wasn't his son. The photo was old, a Polaroid from decades ago.

"My brother Robbie," said Thurston.

Sandra felt as though she should say something about Robbie—how attractive he was or how much he looked like Thurston, or else, she might ask where or when the picture was taken. She didn't, though, because she was anxious to get to the subject of the final exam and her grade in Thurston's course. She had questions, she wanted to tell him, and he was refusing to let her ask them. The way he treated her in class was unacceptable, she planned to say. She struggled to organize her thoughts. She opened her mouth to speak.

"He's dead," said Thurston abruptly.

"What?" Sandra caught her breath.

"Robbie is dead. My Lai."

He looked as though his milkstone veneer were going to shatter. He peered at her with unblinking eyes as if to make sure she had understood. War had taken his brother. If he was a pacifist, it was for a reason. She peered back to let him know she had. Then suddenly,

Sandra's mind jerked alert, and her thoughts began to spin like windmills. It was a lie, she said to herself. The old bastard was trying to manipulate her. Robbie couldn't have died at My Lai.

"I thought all the casualties were Vietnamese," she said coolly.

Professor Thurston stared at her as if she were a dolt.

"In a war," he said glacially, "there are different kinds of casualties."

Sandra cocked her head.

"Suicide," he said, and Sandra realized his voice was quivering. "Some of them just couldn't live with it."

That's all she told me about her visit with Professor Thurston, but I had the impression that nothing had been resolved.

* * *

Christmas was approaching and, with it, final exams. The sun, a giant pearl, hung low in a stone-white sky. The holly bush outside my front window flaunted its festive berries. Most of my boarders planned to fly home to visit their families. Some were leaving for good to take jobs in distant cities after the first of the year. I was baking tarts and primping the house in preparation for the holidays.

During it all, Sandra studied. She left early in the morning for the library, book-laden briefcase in hand, and returned after midnight, when the moon shone opalescent in the sky.

One evening, when I returned home from work, I noticed that Sandra's door was ajar. It was unusual for her to be back so early. I peeked in and found her packing, folding her clothes meticulously—jeans, shirts, uniforms, even bras and panties—and placing each item into the suitcase.

I rarely entered the boarders' rooms unless repairs were necessary, and I hadn't seen Sandra's since she'd moved in. Everything was as pristine as the day I had first handed her the key. The bedspread emitted a slightly fruity smell. She must have washed it in citrus-scented laundry detergent. A bouquet of dried flowers stood on the night table alongside a framed photo of Sandra with two other women. Beams of moonlight fell through the window.

"What's going on, Sandra?"

"I'm sorry I couldn't give you notice, Mrs. Montez," she said, "but I have to leave." Her air was cool, unruffled.

My back stiffened. I felt like a guard dog poised to attack an intruder.

"Thurston!" I growled.

"No," she said, smiling. "The Army. They're sending me to Afghanistan."

"A week before finals?"

"That's how it is, Mrs. M. You have to go wherever they send you."

"And whenever?"

"Yes, whenever. I have a couple of days to fly out to Chicago to say good-bye to my mom and grandmother. Then I leave for San Antonio for additional training and from there to Afghanistan. I'll drop you an email if I can."

"But this is crazy! You're almost done with the semester!"

"It's just as well. I can begin my second year again when I come back, maybe somewhere else. At any rate, I won't be taking any more courses with Professor Thurston."

She packed the photo, then closed her suitcase and went to the door.

"Corey said he'd drive me to the airport," she said. Corey Frater had been one of my first boarders, and he was still with me. "Listen, Mrs. M., I know this is sudden. I already paid for December, but I want to pay for January too. You shouldn't lose a month of income."

"No need, Sandra. Just stay safe."

She hugged me and left.

* * *

Crocuses were blooming. The winter sky shimmered like ribbons of turquoise crepe. It was Saturday and the house was quiet. I turned on the computer and smiled. Sandra had written from Kabul. She would soon be shipping off to somewhere remote. She was happy, she said. She was learning a lot and working side-by-side with doctors, doing what she had been trained to do.

She didn't mention Thurston. Maybe she had put the whole business behind her. I thought she probably had. She wasn't one to dwell on the past.

Prejudice

"Kill the Jews!" Sami quipped amicably. He smiled at Lt. Schwarzman and stuck out his hand. "Money?"

Schwarzman tightened his jaw and stared Sami right in the eye, but there was no sign of hostility in the Iraqi's gaze.

"What did you say?" asked Schwarzman coolly.

"Let it go," whispered Morales. "That's just the way he greets people."

"Are you kidding?"

Lt. Schwarzman thought he knew something about Iraq. He'd majored in Arabic and spoke it pretty fluently. He'd read dozens of books in addition to the ones he'd been assigned in Officer Candidate School. He talked to Iraqis, not just soldiers and police but ordinary citizens—carpenters, tailors, barbers. Sunnis and Shiites. But he'd only heard someone utter those words once before—on a base in Ramadi. He'd been in charge of payroll there too.

"Name and ID," said Schwarzman.

"Sami al-Hamedi," said the soldier, still

smiling broadly. "You speak Arabic pretty well for an American. Very nice!"

Schwarzman gave him an envelope.

"Why don't you pay in dollars instead of dinar?" joked Sami. "Then I could get rich and go to California!"

Schwarzman glowered and checked off Hamedi's name.

"*As-salaamu alaykum,*" he said to the next soldier without looking back at Sami. He fingered through the box of envelopes and paid the man.

"Can't believe I'm risking my life for these anti-Semitic bastards," muttered Aaron Schwarzman.

"It's just something they learn," Morales assured him. "They repeat it over and over mindlessly. It's like saying 'God bless you' when someone sneezes. Do you really mean to pray for the guy who's just sprayed you with germs?"

"Or 'adios.'"

"Exactly," said Morales. "You probably don't care whether the asshole 'goes with God' or the devil."

"Or fuck you," snickered Schwarzman sourly.

"Now you've got the idea," laughed Morales. "You're not actually wishing somebody a good screw when you say that, are you? Well, it's the same with them. They've got these phrases they use all the time. They don't think about what they mean. In fact, they don't even *know* what they mean."

"Yeah, but if they keep saying it and teach their kids to say it…"

"Prejudice dies hard, that's true. Back home they still call me 'the Mexican,' even though my family came to California in 1911 during the Mexican Revolution. When I go to vote, they hand me a ballot in Spanish. Sure, I'm proud of my Mexican heritage and all that, but sometimes I ask myself, how deep do your roots have to be in the U.S. before you're considered a real American? When I tell people I'm a Marine, they assume I went in because I was too dumb to go to college, even though I have a degree in psychology from U.C.L.A."

"But that son of a bitch wishes I were dead!"

"Don't sweat it, Aaron. He doesn't know anything about you. To him, Aaron Schwarzman is just another American name, like Jack Smith. Actually, Sami's a pretty good guy… and a damn good soldier. We were in a joint operation in Mosul."

Schwarzman walked across the yard,

where Iraqi recruits were booting a ball from one to the other. He sat down at a desk and started writing up a report, but he couldn't get Sami's words out of his head. Kill the Jews? "Why, you bastard?" he asked himself. "Why?"

Somebody always wanted to kill the Jews. Aaron had grown up hearing his father's stories about murder and death camps. One of the reasons he'd joined the Marines was to get away from those stories. But there was no getting away. The images kept coming back.

* * *

November 9, 1938. Munich. Glass shattering. Windows exploding like fireworks. Shards hurling through space, slamming into furniture, walls, faces. Screams—head-piercing, heart-piercing screams—and crashing. Sledgehammers against walls. Concrete crumbling. Light fixtures shattering. More screams. Detonations. Blood. A small child crouching under a sewing table, shivering, holding his breath, struggling not to cough, not to urinate, not to breathe. A handsome young man in his prime, clear, bright eyes, a handlebar mustache, firm jaw, straight (not hooked) nose, sandy hair: Abel Schwarzman, Aaron's grandfather. Aaron had never seen him, except in photos. The comely young man was still clutching a swatch of fabric when thugs in brown shirts thundered into his tailor shop and grabbed him by the collar.

"Kill the Jews!" One shot and Abel Schwarzman lay oozing blood onto the cobblestones. The hoodlums smashed the sewing machines, the mannequins, the mirrors, even the canary in its cage. They carried off the cash and as much cloth as they could. They did not notice Abel's six-year-old son, Heinrich, hiding in the shadows.

Once the streets were calm, Heinrich groped his way home. He found the apartment unlocked and tiptoed in. "Ima! Ima!" he called softly. But his Ima wasn't in the kitchen or in the sewing room. He peeped into the bedroom, terrified of what he might see, but there was only a deathly emptiness. Hands trembling, he pried open the armoire. Her clothes hung in an orderly row, but where was Ima? Not there, not under the bed, not in the bathroom. Heinrich began to whimper and then to panic.

He darted through the front door and scuttled to his Tante Louisa's house. His aunt heard his garbled relation and decided she was not going to wait for the roundup. She wrote a note for her husband, stuffed as much cash and jewelry as she could into her underwear, and made her way to the train station, where she boarded a train headed south, little Heinrich and her own two children, Leah and Hermann, in tow.

Somewhere in the mountains the train stopped. Louisa didn't know whether they were in Switzerland or still in Germany, but as soon as she heard the stomp of boots on the floor of an adjacent car, she shoved her way to the door and took off through the woods with her three small charges.

Louisa did not share the fascination of her countrymen with the forest. She saw it neither as a refuge nor a spiritual haven. From fairy tales she knew the woods teemed with wolves and spirits, and so she forced the children to trudge through the muck for hours, until at last, they came to a clearing. Louisa looked around, trying to figure out which way to go. The children were exhausted and hungry, but Louisa was afraid of villages housing thugs and even more afraid of the tangle of vegetation, with its fierce creatures and poisonous berries. Suddenly, she felt a hand like a vise on her shoulder. One of the children, probably Leah, let out a cry, and Louisa instinctively reached out her hand to muzzle her.

"Shh!" ordered their captor, nodding slightly and signaling her to follow.

The woman gradually released her grip. Louisa stared at her, wide-eyed. The children gaped in terror. It seemed they were in the custody of a nun. She wore a long, black dress with a wide, white collar, and on her head, a large, starched cornette like a dove with outstretched wings. Her skin was furrowed and as crinkly as crepe paper, but she had a sturdy torso and a powerful gait.

"We are Sisters of Charity," she explained simply. "We take care of people like you." Her voice was throaty and detached. She led the little band over an invisible path through the forest to a small, stone building. A large flag with a swastika hung over the front door, and Louisa realized they were still in Germany.

"I am Sister Jutta," said the nun. "You are welcome to stay with us if you like. If you do, the children will attend school and learn a craft. You will work in the laundry room or wherever there is need."

Tante Louisa was the wife of Abraham Schwarzman, a successful dry goods merchant. She was accustomed to having a maid fold her laundry and serve her tea in a porcelain cup, but she bit her lip, bowed her head, and thanked the nun.

"Another thing," said Sister Jutta. "You will all learn Christian prayers. In case of a raid, you must be able to pass for members of our community. You will wear a habit, and the children will wear school uniforms."

"Yes, ma'am," whispered Tante Louisa.

"Yes, *Sister*," the nun corrected her. "Also, here there are no special rituals—you know what I mean—and no special foods. You are welcome to share what we have, but as for kosher…"

"Of course, Sister." And then, after a pause, "Is there… is there any way I could contact my husband, Abraham, to let him know—"

"Certainly not!" snapped Sister Jutta. "You would put not only yourself but all of us in danger!" She turned to Heinrich and Hermann, shaking her head and sighing. Tiny veins like entwined spider webs traversed her cheeks. "I suppose the boys have been circumcised," she said grimly. "Well, there's nothing we can do about it. We'll just have to take the risk. Let's just pray to Jesus the Nazis don't pull down their trousers to check."

* * *

"She didn't seem very happy to have us

there," Heinrich told his son years later. They were sitting on a park bench in New York, feeding popcorn to the pigeons. "She was matter-of-fact, never warm."

"Maybe she thought the Nazis were right," muttered Aaron.

"No, that was just her way." After a moment of silence, he added, "It was thanks to those nuns that we survived. I'm profoundly grateful. That's why I send them a donation once a month, and when I die, Aaron, I want you to continue the practice."

"And Uncle Abraham?" asked Aaron. "What happened to him?"

"Oh, Tante Louisa shouldn't have worried about contacting him. He was dead by the time we got to the convent. Bludgeoned to death in his doorway, is what the neighbors told me when I went back after the war to try to find him."

Aaron didn't ask about his grandmother. He knew his father had never been able to find her. She had disappeared without a trace.

"The nun gave Tante Louisa a novice's habit—white with a plain white veil—and put her to work washing bedclothes," explained Heinrich. "Then she led Leah, Hermann, and me to the schoolroom—a dingy hall filled with traumatized children wearing blue shirts and gray pants or skirts." He sank into thought. "Eventually we learned to play again. Amazing, isn't it? We learned to laugh, even in those horrible circumstances. We were children, after all."

"Did the Nazis ever come?"

"Once. We were in the chapel reciting the rosary. They stood at the altar staring into our faces, trying to determine which of the boys looked nervous. Those were the ones they were going to pull out and examine. Finally, they nabbed Johann Schiller and Christian Frondizi. Both of them were country boys from nearby villages and they had their foreskins. The Nazis would have continued their investigation, but Sister Jutta suddenly turned to face them, hurling a glare like a grenade. *'Kommen Sie mit mir,'* she commanded in her no-nonsense way. She led them to the refectory, where I imagine she gave them a good dinner with lots of beer and sent them packing."

* * *

Aaron stared at the computer screen and began to write his report: "Fifty-four Iraqi recruits received pay in the amount of…" But why? he thought. Why did they say, "Kill the Jews"? And when would people ever stop thinking that way? The War had ended nearly fifty years ago. Sometime in 1946 Aaron's father, aunt, and cousins made their way to France and then to New York. Miraculously, Louisa raised two boys and a girl by herself, first working as a seamstress and then as a hat designer for Lilly Daché. Heinrich married Adele Bloom, the American-born daughter of a Holocaust survivor. He became a successful New York attorney and president of the advisory board at the local synagogue. He even fought in Vietnam.

"Why did you go?" Aaron once asked him. "You were a student. You could have gotten out of it. It was a shitty war."

"We didn't know it was a shitty war. Anyhow, I thought the government would pay for law school."

Aaron knew the real reason why Heinrich had gone to Vietnam: because in the recesses of his mind, he was still that tiny boy cowering under the sewing table in his father's tailor shop. He went because he was a Jew, and everyone thought that Jews ran away. He had to prove that he could face the enemy and fight.

"I'm tired of the victimhood shit. Get over it, Dad," Aaron said under his breath. "There are no Brown Shirts over here."

In college, Aaron enrolled in political

science. Then, on September 11, 2001, he watched a plane fly into the Pentagon from the roof of his residence hall. He watched American flags being burned on TV. Enough, he thought. He changed his major to Arabic—to understand the foe better, he said—and filled out the forms for Officer Candidate School. The day after his graduation, he was commissioned as a second lieutenant in the Marines.

"I'm not going to war to prove that Jews can fight," he told his father. "I'm going because I want to serve. My country needs me."

"They won't let you forget that you're a Jew," said Heinrich Schwarzman, tears streaming down his cheeks. He sank onto the sofa. "Don't go, Aaron," he sobbed. "Enough war. You don't have to do this."

His mother was so upset she locked herself in the bedroom.

Aaron left for Marine Corps Base Quantico in June 2004. That's where he met Al Morales, and he knew from the beginning they were kindred spirits.

"There's no black or white in the Marines," the training sergeant proclaimed on the first day of boot camp. "Only green. All Marines are the same color: green."

"Bullshit," whispered a broad-shouldered black kid standing next to Aaron.

But for Aaron it turned out to be pretty much true. Nobody hassled him because his name was Aaron Schwarzman and he'd been bar mitzvahed. All that mattered was that he had the smarts and the upper body strength to pass the tests. And, of course, Arabic was a plus for an infantryman. Aaron felt liberated. He was appreciated for what he knew and what he could accomplish. The burden of his father's demons had been lifted… he thought.

* * *

Aaron finished writing his payroll report and went to find something to eat.

"You know," Sami said when he returned the following month to collect his salary, "at my former base in Ramadi, there was a guy who handed out the envelopes… he was a lot like you. They called him 'The Jew.'"

"Yeah?"

"He was real tight-fisted. Never let a dinar slip through the cracks. Accounted for every coin. Never took a bribe. You couldn't put a thing past him."

"That's why you called him 'The Jew'? Because he was honest?"

"But honesty is not always such a good

thing, you know. I mean, it's not natural. It's not how things work." Sami stared at Schwarzman. "Hey, that guy was you, right? You're The Jew!"

"Yeah," said Morales through the interpreter. "He's the one. Listen, Sami, have you ever actually seen a Jew?"

"A real Jew? No…"

"Sure about that?" interrupted Schwarzman. "Would you know one if you saw one?"

"Yeah, of course. They have big hook noses and beady eyes."

"Why do you want to kill them? Why do you always say, 'Kill the Jews'?"

"Because they control all the money in the world. The only reason you Americans are here is because Israel is paying the U.S. to take over Iraq, so that Iraq will buffer Israel against Iran. It's all about Jewish money."

"That's ridiculous, Sami. We're here to fight Al-Qaida."

"Because Al-Qaida wants to destroy Israel. Like I said, Jewish money."

"Well, why are *you* fighting this war, Sami?"

"Oh, Al-Qaida, they're real mean guys. They do horrible things. They behead people for nothing." Then he snickered. "And besides, you pay me. Like I said, Jewish money."

"Good-bye, Sami."

"Good-bye, friend. Kill the Jews!"

* * *

The next time Schwarzman found himself arm's length from Sami, they were both crouching behind a half-burned-out tower on the roof of a besieged building. It had once been part of a government office complex with long, graceful colonnades, arched doorways, and elaborately decorated ceilings. Insurgents occupied it early in the war. They fired on civilians from blown-out windows and converted the sumptuous meeting rooms into munitions storerooms. American bombs had reduced the ornate stone- and woodwork to rubble, but most of the exterior structure still stood. Now Al-Qaida was battling to get it back, but the building's strategic location made the Americans determined to hold onto it. The Marines and their Iraqi partners were camped out on the roof and the upper floors. Sami and Aaron crouched by the ledge while two Marine corporals, Bob Lincoln and Ross Kaminsky, occupied positions behind pillars. A barrage of fire came from the east, apparently from the shattered upper-floor window of a former dentist's office. Then another and another, each from a different location.

"Shit," whispered Aaron, "they're everywhere."

There was a pause in the shelling. Schwarzman tensed and squinted at the horizon. For once Sami wasn't grinning.

A man wearing a black *keffiyeh* appeared in a doorway. Ross took aim.

"Wait," whispered Sami in Arabic. "He's a decoy. Let's see what he does."

But Sami wasn't looking at the man. His eyes were focused on the roof of a building opposite the one they were defending.

Ross inched closer to the edge for a better view of the street.

"No!" screamed Sami. "Get back!"

But before Aaron could translate, a sniper's bullet had begun its trajectory. "Down!" Sami screamed. In the split second it took for the projectile to reach its mark, Sami had leaped up and pushed Ross to the ground. Then, with a shriek and a gasp, he fell on top of him.

The gash in his shoulder was a geyser of blood and bone.

"Keep doing what you're doing!" Aaron yelled at the men. "Richter!" he called to the radio operator through a hole in the floor. "Get Balad! We need an air ambulance!"

"They can't land here, Lieutenant!"

"They can land on the terrace in back."

"It's dangerous!"

"No kidding! War is dangerous!"

"Andrews!" he shouted to the sergeant through the same hole. "Get up here and help me!"

Aaron fashioned a makeshift dressing out of his shirt and gauze from the first aid kit and placed it on Sami's wound. He bore down on Sami's body with all of his weight to stem the bleeding. Then he threw a blanket over him because in spite of the heat, hypothermia was a danger.

"I've got to get him out of here! What does Balad say?"

"Twenty minutes!"

"In twenty minutes, he could be dead!"

Aaron stretched Sami out on a kind of raised loggia, covered except for an open surface that had once been adorned with potted plants, at the back of the building. He was sure there was enough room for a copter to land.

* * *

"You know," Morales told Sami when he visited him, "you're a fucking war hero. You saved Ross Lincoln's life." Morales turned to the interpreter. "Can you tell him that for me, please?"

Morales was sitting by Sami's bed at the medical facility in Balad.

Sami grinned. "Kill the Jews!" he said weakly.

"Do you know that Aaron Schwarzman is a hero too?" Morales said. "He saved *your* life. It's thanks to him that you didn't bleed to death."

"Good man," whispered Sami. "I love Lt. Schwarzman. Where is he? Why didn't he come?"

"He finished his tour. They sent him back to the States. Listen, Hamedi," Morales said gently. "I want to tell you something. Something that will surprise you."

"You're giving me a plane ticket to California?"

"Aaron Schwarzman is Jewish."

Sami stared at Morales blankly. He obviously hadn't understood.

"It's true," insisted Morales. "Schwarzman is a Jew."

"No," said Sami, shaking his head. "You're teasing me." He let out a little chuckle, even though his chest hurt when he laughed.

"I'm not teasing," said Morales, looking Sami right in the eye.

Sami lay there, shaking his head. He seemed to be struggling to absorb the meaning of Morales's words.

"I know a Jew when I see one," he said finally. "Jews have hooked noses and beady eyes." He smiled amicably. "Thanks for coming, Lieutenant Morales. Kill the Jews!"

Morales took a breath to say something, but Sami had closed his eyes and sunk into his pillow. In a minute or two, he was sound asleep.

Who the Hell is Rosie Méndez?

The first time I walked into the mess hall, I felt like a ham sandwich. They all leered at me, mouths watering as if they wanted to take a bite. Soldiers are supposed to show self-control. They gave us a lecture about it during training. Soldiers are supposed to be poker-faced, detached. Apparently, these guys didn't get the memo though, because their mouths were watering like starving Iraqi dogs that had just caught the whiff of meat. Not American dogs, because over here dogs get fed. Over there, they wander through the streets, hoping some GI left a piece of jerky in the garbage. That's the way these guys were looking at me: like a morsel they couldn't wait to get their paws on.

"Hey, sugar," one of them called. "Come sit by me!"

"Come over here, darlin'!"

"Come on, Rosie, there's a place at my table!"

I looked around to see if I could spot another woman, but there were no free seats near any of my girlfriends. I put down my tray at the end of a table by the food line. A couple of guys snickered. A huge black man smiled and waved at me. He had a scar on his cheek and the name Kavanagh written in black letters across his pocket.

"Hey, sweetheart!" yelled Kavanagh. "Let's go dancing tonight!"

I laughed. We all knew that the rest of the day we'd be in combat training, then sports, then dinner, then meetings with our teams.

"Right," I said. "I'll wear my evening gown and a tiara!"

I smiled and looked down at my meatloaf. I knew the bantering and teasing were all part of the game. They warned us in training that you just had to go along with it. If you were standoffish, the guys would make your life miserable. If you were flirty, they'd think you were easy. I didn't like it though. I didn't like feeling as though they were all ready to devour me. It reminded me of what had happened before. I joined the Army to get away from all that, but I was beginning to think that the base wasn't that different from Boyle Heights.

* * *

The house in Boyle Heights was nicer than the one in San Teófanes. Back in El Salvador, we had only two rooms—a bedroom and a kind of all-purpose space that served as a kitchen, a living room, and everything else. There was no plumbing. We used an outhouse. But living conditions weren't the reason we left. We left because of the violence, the marauding FMLA soldiers—leftist guerrillas—who barged into yards and stole your only cow, your only shovel, and whatever else you had.

On the morning they kicked in our door, I was playing in the bedroom with a plastic doll my mother had bought for me at Don Tello's, the only store in San Teófanes. I was four years old. It's a good thing I was in the house and not in the yard. Otherwise, who knows what would have happened? Mamá shoved me under the bed so they wouldn't see me. She was trembling and crying and trying to get away, but five or six men encircled her. From under the bed I could see their black boots and smell their oily, tobacco-saturated bodies. I saw one of the soldiers get very close to Mamá and pull up her skirt, but that's all I saw because I closed my eyes, slid back against the wall, and made myself into a ball. Mamá let out the most horrible, bloodcurdling scream I'd ever heard, a scream as sharp as an ax. Then she was quiet. When I crept out from under the bed, she was lying on the floor, blood oozing from her mouth and ear. Her eyes were as swollen as Tío José's goiter, and angry bruises blackened her shoulders and arms. One of the soldiers had stuffed her panties into her mouth. I felt my saliva turn to vinegar.

When my father came back from the fields, I ran to him, sobbing.

"Papá," I spluttered. "They've hurt Mami."

He found her crumbled on a chair, pressing a compress against her engorged lip. He stood there staring at her a long while, his jaw tight, his eyes squinty. Suddenly, he threw his canteen on the ground. It exploded like a bomb.

"*Puta!*" he screamed. "You whore!"

"No, Papá, no!" I tried to grab his hand, but he pushed me away with such force that I landed on the ground.

"How did you let them touch you, you whore! You probably loved it!"

"Alberto," Mami sobbed. "No..."

"This only happens because women want it, Verónica!"

Papá raised his hand behind his head, like my brother Paco when he was getting ready to pitch a baseball. When he brought it down on the side of Mami's skull, the thud threw me back onto the floor. It sounded like a clap of thunder. Mami's ear was bleeding again.

"I'm not living with some whore," he snarled. He spat at her and tramped out the door. It was the last time I ever saw him.

Jaime and Paco got back from school around lunchtime.

"Mami!" wailed Paco. "What happened?" He was only seven, and all he could do was sit on the floor and bawl.

Jaime, who was eleven, knew what had happened. "They raped her," he said with chilling indifference. He was only a child, but he already had the hardened features of an adult, and he knew what a man could do to a woman.

That was the first time I ever heard the word *rape*. I wasn't sure what it meant, but I vowed I'd never let it happen to me.

That night we went to Tío José's house. Mami's older brother was a soft-spoken, clear-thinking man, a widower who had raised seven children on his own after his wife had died of cancer. All three of his daughters lived in Los Angeles, and one of them—Luci, the youngest—had managed to go to a vocational school and now worked as a dental assistant.

"You have to leave here," said Tío José.

"The soldiers will be back, and so will Alberto."

"But where will we go? I have no money." Mami touched her lip gingerly. I could tell it was still hurting her.

"North like everybody else. You can stay with Luci in Los Angeles until you get settled."

Almost half the village of San Teófanes had already left for the United States. They sold their pigs, their kitchen utensils, their wheelbarrows, and their shoes—whatever they had—to put cash together for the trip. But Mami didn't have that kind of time. She had to raise money immediately. Who knew when Alberto or the soldiers might reappear?

"For the four of you, it will be at least eight hundred dollars," Tío José mused. "I can give you three hundred. I've been saving." He looked down at his hands, which made his goiter swell up like a bullfrog's.

Mami's cheeks were moist. "I couldn't accept your money," she whispered.

"Take it, Vero. I've been saving up to go myself, but I'm too old. I want you to go. For the sake of the children. Let them make something of themselves, like Luci."

Luci was his pride and joy, the educated daughter who had a good job.

"Stay here tonight," said Tío José. "Tomorrow we'll find a solution."

Don Tello had made a fortune working with coyotes to smuggle Salvadorans into the United States, and within a week he managed to get us on the truck that would take us through Guatemala to the Mexican border. From there, we began the harrowing journey through Chiapas and Oaxaca, where border guards and bandits demanding money intercepted us at every turn. When at last we got to Texas, we divided into groups. The coyote stuffed Mami, the boys, and me into the hidden compartment of a car. The police searched the vehicle, but somehow we made it across to El Paso. From there we caught a bus to Los Angeles, where Cousin Luci met us at the terminal and took us to her house in her car. Her very own car. A Hyundai. Of all the marvelous things Cousin Luci possessed, the one that fascinated me most was the car. Even then, I loved engines.

Mamá took the usual jobs—hotel maid, dishwasher, babysitter. When she learned enough English, she sold tickets in a movie theater and shampooed ladies' hair in a beauty shop. Eventually she paid off her loan from Don Tello and rented a little house in Boyle Heights. Now we had running water, flush toilets, regular phone service, and a TV, just like Cousin Luci. We even had our own little garden where we could plant vegetables and a porch where we could sit and listen to the *corridos* from the bar across the street.

To tell the truth, it wasn't really that different from San Teófanes. Instead of FMLA soldiers, there were gangs. Instead of guerrillas, there were drug dealers. Gunfire in the night, just like back home. Screams and pleas, wailing and funerals and dead children, just like back home. Blood on the street. Tears and more tears. We came to Boyle Heights to get away from San Teófanes, and I joined the Army to get away from Boyle Heights.

I was fourteen when I made the decision to leave. That afternoon I was in the kitchen stuffing *pupusas* with ground pork. A *pupusa* is a kind of tortilla made of thick corn dough, and you can fill it with almost anything. The pork was frying on a low flame, and the aroma of chili, cilantro, and cumin filled the kitchen. Suddenly, I heard someone come in through the front door. I thought it must be Jaime. My oldest brother was not following in Cousin Luci's footsteps, as Mamá had hoped. He was twenty-one already, but he hadn't finished school and still didn't have a regular job. He seemed to be staggering in a windstorm, propelled by gusts and thrusts, with no focus or control.

"Jaime?" I called from the kitchen. I stepped toward the door, a spatula in my hand.

He wasn't alone. He was with two other young men—one heavyset and dark, with a thin mustache and a heavy gold chain around his neck, the other, slimmer and fair-skinned, with long hair tied back in a messy ponytail. They were arguing.

Jaime turned and saw me. "Get out of here!" he snapped.

Obviously, I'd interrupted something. I ducked back into the kitchen and started cutting yucca into thick, round slices. Afterward, I would prepare a *curtido* of cabbage, onions, and carrots to spoon on top. Mamá wouldn't be home from her job at the beauty shop until about eight, but I'd have dinner ready way before then. Paco had to eat as soon as he got home from school because he was in a band and had a rehearsal that night.

The men were screaming in the next room. "You gotta pay!" "You'll get your money! Wait a few days!" "Now, motherfucker!" "Two more days, man!" "You gotta pay!" "I will! I promise!" "Now, motherfucker! You gotta pay now!"

I was scared somebody was going to pull a gun. Maybe I should call the police, I thought, but I knew my brother would kill me if I did. We had green cards; it wasn't that. But if the police came and arrested any of them for dealing drugs, that would be an act of treachery Jaime would never forgive. I looked down at the knife in my hand and began to tremble. Instinctively, I hid it in a drawer under a pot holder.

"You don't got the money, then give us back the stuff!" one of the men howled.

"I don't have it," pleaded Jaime. "But I'll get the money."

"Give us something else! That TV set, for example."

"I can't! It's my mother's."

"Aw, it's his mommy's. I don't want that piece of crap anyhow. What else you got that's worth something?"

All of a sudden the guy with the long hair burst into the kitchen. "Hey! Who the hell is this?" he yelled to the other thug. "How about it, Jaime, want to give us your little sister?"

Jaime stood staring at him, as if drunk.

"Hey, little girl," hissed the blond guy. He came closer. I could see the enlarged pores on his nose and smell the weed on his breath.

"Well, Jaime?"

I expected Jaime to jump the guy, to pummel him with his fists, to grab a cutting board and smash it over his head. Instead, he just stood in the doorway, staring. The big, mustached man pushed past him into the kitchen.

My blood was turning to needles in my veins. I regretted having put away the knife. The blond guy grabbed my wrist. His grip was like a vise. I winced.

"How about it, Jaime?"

But Jaime just shrugged and left the room.

I struggled to kick the guy in the shins, but the other one came around behind me and grabbed me in a choke hold. They pushed me down, and my head felt as though it were shattering as it hit the floor. One held me fast while the other thrust himself into me. Then they changed places. I don't know how many times they did it. It was as though I was dead.

When I opened my eyes, they were gone. Paco was kneeling beside me, sobbing.

"Oh, God," he cried. "First Mami and now you. Please don't die, Rosie. Please don't die." He kissed my hand over and over. "Please, little sister. Please don't die."

I struggled for breath and squeezed his wrist. Finally, I whispered, "I'm okay,

Paquito. I'm going to be okay."

"Are you in pain?"

Of course I was in pain, but more than pain what I felt was rage. Rage at the thugs. Rage at Jaime. Rage at God for making men the way they are.

Not all men, of course. Paco was different. He picked me up and carried me to my room. Then he put me in bed.

"I'm getting out of here," I spluttered. "Out of this house. Out of this neighborhood."

"Not yet, little sister. You have to grow up first. You have to finish school." How could Paco be so good when Jaime was so useless? I wondered. Paco was all set to enroll in college after high school. He was going to study computer technology and make something of himself like Cousin Luci.

"You're a good student, Rosie," he pressed on. "Your English is great. Don't give it all up."

"I just want to leave," I moaned.

When Mamá came home and saw me, she crumpled onto the sofa and sobbed. Then she went into the kitchen, found the knife, and finished preparing the yucca. She didn't call the police, even though the television set was missing.

I did finish high school, but the day after

graduation, I went down to the recruiting office and enlisted. The Army seemed like the surest way to get out of town, and anyway, I didn't want to go to college. I wanted to be a mechanic, and the recruitment officer said there was a training program for mechanics opening up. Once I got on base though, they convinced me to sign up for laundry specialist. That means washerwoman. I didn't argue. I was just glad they took me.

* * *

I had no idea what it would be like to be one of two hundred women on a base of forty-five hundred soldiers.

"Hey, Méndez!" called Kavanagh from the other end of the lunch table. He knew my name because it was written on my left breast pocket, just like everyone else's. "You like to mambo?"

"I bet she can really wiggle her ass!" said the guy sitting next to him.

"Don't be crude," snapped Kavanagh.

The laundry was boring. Every time I had a spare moment, I ran to the garage, where the mechanics were servicing the trucks. I hung around and watched. Before long, I knew what a glow plug was and the difference between an oil cooler hose and a water hose. I asked questions. I learned how to install a

Haldex air dryer on a 5-ton truck and how to rebuild a 25-amp generator.

"Hey, girl," one of the sergeants snapped at me. "You're not supposed to be here. Get lost."

I turned to leave.

"I'm talking to you, girl!"

"Yes, I'm going."

"Yes, Sergeant Brenner!"

"Yes, Sergeant Brenner, I'm going."

But whenever I could, I snuck back. I was fascinated with trucks.

One day, Kavanagh stuck his head out from under a huge cargo vehicle.

"Hey, beautiful," he said with a grin. "You looking for me?"

"You crazy, Kavanagh? I didn't even know you worked over here."

"Jim Kavanagh, Master Mechanic, at your service. Stick around, baby. I'll teach you a few things." He made his voice sound sexy, but I knew he was teasing.

"You know," I overheard him say to Brenner one day just as I was coming into the garage, "Rosie Méndez has a real head for this stuff. Maybe you could get her transferred over here."

"Who the hell is Rosie Méndez?"

"She's that pretty little black-haired

Latina. They've got her over there washing bedsheets, but maybe you could talk to someone about a transfer."

After the sergeant left, I went into the shop. "I heard what you told Brenner," I said to Jim. "That was real nice of you."

A couple of days later, as I was leaving the laundry, Brenner called me over.

"Listen, Méndez," he said. "I hear you want to be a mechanic. Maybe I could talk to somebody about getting you into a training program."

I couldn't believe my good luck. "That would be wonderful!" I gasped.

"You'll have to meet with the job counselor and fill out an application. If you've got time, I'll walk you over to the office."

About halfway down the corridor, Brenner pushed open the door to the stairwell.

"I thought it was down at the end of the hall," I said.

"Yeah, it is, but I just want to explain something to you before we get there." He grabbed my arm and yanked me through the door.

My senses were suddenly on full alert. The stairwell was empty. If he tried something and I screamed, he'd gag me. The hideous memory of Mamá lying on the floor with her panties stuffed into her mouth flickered in my brain. And then, the memory of Jaime's friends.

"Don't get all fidgety," he said softly. "I just want to talk to you." His veins bulged under the skin of his milky-white forehead. He was still clutching my arm.

"I want to go to the jobs office."

He tried to make his voice sound soothing. "You have to understand, Rosie, we already have enough mechanics. In the Army, you have to work where we need you, which may not be exactly where you want to go."

"But you said I could apply to be reassigned."

"Well, the job counselor is a friend of mine. I could talk to him. But, of course, you'd have to be nice to me."

"What do you mean?" I knew what he meant.

He let go of my arm and suddenly shoved me face-first against the wall. He covered my mouth with one hand and grabbed my breast with the other. Then he began to work his fingers into my shirt.

The old rage surged through my body. I stomped backward on his boot and wrenched myself free. He lunged toward me, and I took advantage of the thrust of his body to propel him further off balance. As he struggled to steady himself, I rammed against him with the full weight of my body. Nothing fancy. Just stuff I'd learned in boot camp. He stumbled and went plunging headlong down the stairs.

"You want to know who the hell Rosie Méndez is?" I called after him. "I'm Rosie Méndez."

In the job counselor's office, I filled out an application. By the time I deployed to Iraq in 2004, I was a trained mechanic. At my base in Balad, they assigned me to the team in charge of cargo trucks.

Ox

My son Ignacio never told me much about his tours in Iraq. Nothing about the grenade that Al-Qaida lobbed into his compound, ripping open the roof of the garage. Nothing about the roadside bomb that killed one of his men and cost two others their limbs. Not a word about the medal he won for pulling two Marines out of a burning truck. I heard about all those things from other folks or sometimes from the newspaper. Ignacio did tell me about Ox, though. He even sent me a couple of pictures. Now, when I think back about those hellish times, I give thanks that Ox was there to give comfort.

* * *

Lieutenant Ignacio Montez glared at the sign outside the mess hall and scowled.

"What do you think about this, Ox? Pretty absurd, huh?"

Ox stared at Montez intently, his huge brown eyes unblinking, his muscular body poised for action.

"Come here and look at this, Ox."

Ox's smooth, brown face took on a slightly reddish tint in the sunlight. His perfect features gave him a regal look—like some kind of Egyptian deity, thought Ignacio. Ox moved closer to Montez and sat down.

"It says, 'Except for military dogs, no animals permitted on base.'"

Ox looked up at Montez and wagged his tail, unperturbed.

Montez bent over and scratched him behind the ears. Then he picked up a stick. "Wanna play, Ox? Come on, boy! Wanna play?" Montez threw the stick across the yard, and Ox took off after it. He brought it back to Montez and sat down at his feet, waiting for him to throw it again.

Montez read the sign one more time and shook his head. He knew it wasn't a joke. Captain Bari, the commanding officer, had reviewed the rules with all the platoon leaders: The Department of Defense prohibited military personnel in the U.S. Central Command—and that included Iraq—from adopting pets. Only trained military dogs were permitted on base. All others would be destroyed. In other words, shot.

Nevertheless, Marines routinely fished puppies out of garbage cans and snuck them into their barracks. The Iraqi interpreters who worked with the Marines just couldn't understand why these dopey Americans insisted on adopting straggly dogs who served no obvious military purpose. Ignacio Montez, a second lieutenant with forty-six men under his command, was supposed to model respect for regulations and to serve as an example for his soldiers. Yet he was the first to succumb to the charms of a canine seducer. One day, while patrolling the streets of Ramadi, he heard a desperate squeal that seemed to come from a pile of trash. He knew it could be a trap. A heap of debris could hide an IED. However, this heap turned out to be providing cover for a fluffy, coffee-colored fur ball with enormous, chocolate-brown eyes. Montez stuffed it under his flak jacket.

"Give him an MRE," joked Lt. Kaminsky. "They call this crap Meals Ready to Eat, but they don't mention *by whom*! It's really only good for dog food."

"I don't know," said Montez. "I don't want to make him sick."

"Actually, you should get rid of that dog before you get too attached," added Kaminsky thoughtfully. "You know what Bari is gonna do if he sees it."

"Yeah, I know."

"And don't give it a name. That'll only

make things harder."

Ignacio knew Kaminsky was right, but somehow he just kept putting it off. The pup was a fireball. It would dash around the yard and climb up containers, then hurl himself through the air like a meteor. It hid behind chair legs and attacked empty boots, grabbing them by their laces and shaking them as if they were rats. It burrowed under Ignacio's bedding and ambushed his toes or rifled through his supplies and stole MREs.

"Bad dog!" growled Ignacio after the pup had eaten five or six of them.

The pup just glared at him, his short, spindly legs wide apart and his tail twitching, as though raring for a fight. Then he grabbed Ignacio's pant leg and yanked it this way and that. Ignacio tried to kick the pup off, but he had a grip like a vise. Ignacio stooped and scratched it behind the ears. The pup closed its eyes, released the cloth, and snuggled.

He'd grown strong and chesty after just a few weeks of MREs.

"You're as strong as an ox," chuckled Ignacio, "and you look like an ox. I'm going to call you Ox."

One day Ox found a snake. Nobody knew how it got on base, but the desert is full of dangerous creatures, and sometimes they hide in blankets or equipment that get thrown into trucks and hauled back. This was a horned viper, a poisonous critter with two ugly spikes on its head and a sand-colored body. Ox spied it coiled up in the garage under some equipment.

Zach Sutton, a brawny lance corporal from Illinois, was changing the tires on a truck when he noticed Ox crouched by an oilcan, bottom up, head down. He was snarling fiercely. He had an impressive growl for such a small dog, a low-pitched, steady rumble like a war machine.

"Hey, Lt. Montez, sir," called Zach out the door. "You've got to see this, sir!"

"What's gotten into you?" snapped Ignacio when he saw Ox hunkered and howling by the oilcan. "Come out of there!"

Instead Ox stood up and barked, ears back, teeth bared.

"Shit," whispered Ignacio when he saw the viper.

The creature raised its head. Ox prepared to attack.

"No!" yell Ignacio. Ox had grabbed the snake by the throat and was trying to shake it, but a viper is a strong animal. Ignacio pulled out his sidearm and fired, and the snake fell dead on the floor.

"That was reckless," Ignacio told the dog with mock sternness. "A Marine must never be reckless."

Zach crouched down and pulled Ox to him. "You're a brave soldier," he murmured. "That snake could've bitten me. I think Ox should get a medal, sir," he said to Ignacio. "He may have saved my life."

"You may be right, Zach," said Ignacio, petting the dog.

Kaminsky was getting worried. There was sure to be an inspection sometime soon. "You'd better think about what you're going to do with Ox," he told Ignacio. "You should have gotten rid of him before all your men became so attached. Sutton adores that animal. He's going to lose it if anything happens to the dog."

Ignacio sighed. "I know," he said. "You're right."

"Ox hangs out with him in the garage for hours. Whenever that mutt isn't with you, it's with Sutton." Kaminsky paused and bit his lip. "I'm telling you, you're not going to like what Bari does when he finds him."

Ignacio was preparing his men to patrol a dangerous area of Ramadi when the announcement came about Bari's inspection. Zach snatched up Ox, although the dog now weighed about forty pounds.

"Can we hide him on the roof of the garage, sir?"

Ignacio hesitated. "What if he barks?" Ignacio knew Ox would get fussy if a stranger was around.

"I'll go up with him and feed him MREs," said Zach.

Ignacio sighed. He didn't have a lot of options. "Okay," he said, "but do your best to keep him quiet."

Ignacio went out to meet Bari in the yard. The men formed a line. While the CO was performing his inspection, Ignacio prayed that he wouldn't notice that Sutton was missing. He also prayed that Ox would keep still.

Suddenly a siren sounded. Grenades were flying into and over the walls of the compound. The Marines raced to their positions and returned fire. For an instant Ignacio strained to hear a dog barking through the bedlam, but too many other things demanded his attention for him to dwell on Ox. A bomb exploded somewhere on the roof of the building where Sutton had positioned himself, but the only thing that mattered to Ignacio now was repelling the enemy.

At last the machine guns were quiet. The RPGs stopped soaring overhead. Bari was gone. Ignacio climbed up to the roof and looked around. There were massive holes everywhere. Zach and Ox were huddled in a corner, the man more rattled than the dog.

"Shit," said Zach after he got his bearings. "He's a trooper, sir. He crouched right by me and didn't even flinch." Zach forced himself to grin.

Ox got up and walked gingerly around a jagged opening in the roof, then sat down next to Ignacio.

"You're a champ, Ox," said Ignacio. "A real champ."

"Reminds me of my dog Coco," said Zach. "Coco's a big yellow mutt with a gorgeous swishy tail. We don't really have room for a dog like that in our tiny apartment in Chicago, but she followed me home from school one day, and my mom said I could keep her. Company for a lonely boy, she said. No dad. No siblings. But at least I have a dog. The way I see it, I always have a beautiful blond waiting for me in bed at night."

"And with a great tail!" said Ignacio, laughing.

"Yes, sir, with a great tail. I keep a photo of her under my pillow."

Zach hugged Ox and petted him on the head. "You're a pretty dog too," he whispered.

Less than a week later, Ignacio was in his office doing paperwork when the alarm sounded. Roadside bomb. Seven miles from the base. American vehicles hit. Injuries.

In minutes, Ignacio and three other Marines were on the scene. It looked like a truck had run over an IED and exploded. A fire was raging, consuming the front end of the vehicle. Plumes of black smoke disappeared into the amber sky.

"Cover my ass!" screamed Ignacio. He darted across the rubble to the blazing truck and yanked on a body. The foot was stuck behind a piece of metal. With a twist and a tug, Ignacio got it out, although it appeared to be almost severed above the boot. The man was unconscious, but Ignacio thought he was alive. He handed him over to a waiting Marine, who carried him into a building. In the meantime, Ignacio went to work dislodging another casualty from under parts of the door.

"Help me pull him out!" he called to García, a tough, lanky lance corporal from Texas.

García hadn't waited for orders. He was

already hoisting the wreckage off the body. The victim's arm and chest were a bloody mess of flesh and muscle, but the man was breathing. García slung him over his shoulder and carried him off.

Ignacio poked around the debris with his knife. There appeared to be one more body, this one in the driver's seat. Ignacio groped in the ash, his hand covered with a fireproof glove. He felt something, perhaps a bit of uniform, but it was so badly burned that it crumbled at his touch. *Crap*, thought Ignacio. *No one sitting in the front seat could have survived this blast.* He pushed aside the smoldering powder. Then he worked his hands under the body and tugged. At last he pried it loose. The legs were gone. The torso was scorched indigo. The face was so disfigured that it was barely recognizable. Ignacio squinted at what was left of a human being who moments before had laughed and thought and breathed. He gagged.

"Oh, God," he whispered. "Oh God, no."

It was Zach.

When he got back on base, Ignacio disappeared into the bathroom and retched. Then he crumpled onto the floor. He knew he was supposed to put on a stoic face. He knew he was supposed to pretend he was tough.

But, for now, all he could do was sob. Afterward he would write to Zach's mother. He'd gather up Zach's things, including his photo of Coco, and send them back to her. For now, though, he couldn't bear to think about it. He couldn't bear to think about anything.

By the time he pulled himself together, every-one on base knew what had happened. Kaminsky, who was now Captain Bari's assistant and right-hand man, had called for a helicopter to medivac the two injured Marines to the hospital in Baghdad. One would lose his leg, and the other, his arm, Kaminsky informed Ignacio, but they would survive.

Now Ignacio had to deal with his men. Eighteen- and nineteen-year-olds, kids really. They looked up to him, saw him as an authority figure, and he, at twenty-three, felt like a whimpering toddler, a limp rag. They were all badly shaken. Zach was the platoon's first fatality. The danger after a lethal incident was that soldiers could lose their nerve, and so Ignacio would have to find a way to pump them up again.

He went to talk to each one of them individually. He didn't pretend to be stoic and tough. He let them cry if they wanted to. He let them be the shattered young men they were. Then he called them together. He taught them about different kinds of IEDs and how to dismantle them. He watched as they took them apart, put them back together, and took them apart again. He helped them get over their fear or at least to manage it.

There was little time to grieve. Wars don't halt to give soldiers a couple of weeks to recover from tragedy. Within two days Ignacio's teams of Marines were out patrolling the streets of Ramadi as usual. Only Ox didn't seem to be able to get back to his old routine. He hung around the garage looking for Zach. He sniffed around the trucks where Zach had fixed chassis and changed tires. All the men pampered him and fed him MREs, but Ox seemed inconsolable. He slumped down by Ignacio's feet and stared at him with lonely eyes.

A couple of days later, a team of Marines caught four Al-Qaida operatives hiding weapons in a school and dragged them on base for questioning. Ox crouched by the men and bared his teeth, ears back, tail twitching. It was the same stance he'd taken when he'd cornered the horned viper. He began to snarl.

"At least he knows the good guys from the bad guys," quipped Ignacio.

From then on, every time Ignacio's men brought in insurgents, Ox got mean. He never made a mistake. He knew which ones were Al-Qaida, and he growled and stalked as if he wanted to tear them apart.

Ignacio had to be careful to keep the dog in tow. "The Rules of Engagement forbid undue cruelty," he reminded himself, "even to bastards who hide bombs in schools."

"I'm afraid that one of these days Ox is going to rip one of these motherfuckers apart," Kaminsky told Ignacio. "And then what are you going to tell Bari?"

"I won't let that happen," said Ignacio.

He hadn't seen Kaminsky for a while. As Bari's assistant, Kaminsky was in charge of getting the commanding officer to where he had to go and attend to logistics. Now he was on base to pick up an interpreter for Bari.

"Watch that dog," he told Ignacio when he left. "He's going to get you into trouble."

Kaminsky returned in a week or two. The next time Ignacio saw him, he was standing next to Bari in the yard and announcing an inspection.

"Shit!" shouted Ignacio when he realized what was happening. "Hide the dog! Where is he?"

"He's in the garage, sir!" several of the men shouted back.

"Well, keep him there!"

By now Ox knew the routine, but inexplicably, he began to bark. Ignacio ran to the garage. "Keep him quiet!" he ordered.

"We're trying, sir!" One of the mechanics was trying furiously to rip open an MRE.

But Ox wouldn't stop barking. It was as though he was determined to announce his presence to Bari.

"Quiet!" shouted Ignacio. Then he turned to the men. "Turn on the motors!" he commanded. "Open the back doors and turn on the motors!"

The motors began to roar. One, then another, then another. An earsplitting racket. Yet you could still hear the barking. No matter how many motors they turned on, you could still hear the barking.

Ignacio went out to where Bari and Kaminsky were standing. They had conducted a cursory inspection around the living quarters and were getting ready to leave. Ignacio held his breath.

Then, suddenly, Bari cocked his head and listened. "A dog," he said to Kaminsky. "I thought I heard a dog."

Kaminsky stood silent.

"I'm pretty sure I heard a dog, Lt. Kaminsky. What about you?"

Kaminsky stared right into Bari's eyes.

"No, sir," he said. He pretended to listen very hard. "No, sir," he said again. "I didn't hear a dog."

"No? No dogs here?"

"No, sir. No dogs here."

"Okay," said Bari. "I guess you're right. Let's go."

He and Kaminsky got in their Jeep and drove away.

* * *

By the end of June, Ignacio and his men began preparing to redeploy. Ignacio met with his replacement and introduced him to Ox.

"Take good care of him," he whispered. "He's a good friend and a good Marine."

Ignacio gave Ox one last scratch behind the ears and said good-bye.

Apparently, the new platoon leader took his responsibility seriously, because the last Ignacio heard, Ox was doing fine. Of course, who knows what happened when the Americans left.

* * *

Fourteen months later Ignacio was back in Ramadi, but this time at a training base for Iraqi police. One day, while he was preparing the payroll for the Iraqi recruits, he looked up to see Bari standing in front of him. Ignacio caught his breath.

"Where's the dog?" asked Bari, laughing.

"What dog?" responded Ignacio cautiously. He had, in fact, just pulled two puppies out of the gutter and brought them back for a bath, a good meal, and a comfortable bed.

"Oh, I know you," said Bari. "You've got a dog."

"I don't know what you're talking about." Ignacio had turned as red as a chili.

"No need to worry," said Bari. "I'm not the CO anymore. I don't make inspections these days. Anyhow, give him this. MREs aren't really good for dogs."

He took a bag of Purina out of his rucksack and placed it on Ignacio's desk.

Ignacio opened his mouth but just couldn't think what to say.

Jason's Cap

He seemed pretty much like all the other soldiers to whom I'd rented rooms. Square jaw. Broad shoulders. Reserved demeanor. He was leaving the military, he said. He'd done four tours in Iraq and two in Afghanistan, and he'd served on bases in Texas and Virginia. Now it was time to move on. For the time being he had a job at a bakery, where he was using one of the skills he'd learned in the Army: baking bread. But he was going to study electrical engineering at the local community college. There was nothing wrong with being a baker, he assured me, but he wanted more out of life than that. I liked him. I didn't hesitate for a moment before assigning him the room that had belonged to my eldest daughter, Adriana. She was married now and out of the house. I handed him the keys.

"This one opens the front door, and this one is for your bedroom. Your rent is due the first of the month."

"Okay," he said.

He had a quiet, detached way about him. He picked up his duffle bag.

"There are a few rules at Mrs. Montez's place," I said matter-of-factly when he came down to sign the contract. "Not many, but a few."

"Yeah?" I thought there was a slight smugness to his tone, but I didn't attach any importance to it. The young veterans who rented my rooms had been subjected to so many rules for such a long time that they flinched at the word. Still, when you're a single woman living in a house with a bunch of men, you have to set some limits.

"No smoking in the rooms. No guns or other weapons. No porn in visible places. You can use the kitchen at any time, but aside from coffee, you'll have to supply your own food unless you want to eat dinner here. If you do, let me know the day before. I serve at seven sharp. Be prompt and appropriately dressed. No bare feet. No baseball caps. No rough language at the table. We all treat each other with respect. I think that's it."

He listened without comment. I handed him the contract and watched him sign it: Jason Albemarle. He had a robust signature, with full, clear letters that listed slightly to the right, like hardy sailors steadying themselves against the tilt of the stern. I signed my name by the word "Proprietor": Jacqueline Montez.

"Okay, Jacky," he said, throwing the document and the pen on the table. "See you later."

I raised my eyebrows. "I know I'm a bit old-fashioned," I said calmly, "but I prefer to be called Mrs. Montez. At any rate, I never use the nickname 'Jacky.'" He gawked at me, eyes bulging like hard-boiled eggs. I felt as though I'd asked him to wear a tutu to dinner. "The other young men all call me Mrs. Montez," I said dryly. "Of course, I will be glad to address you any way you want."

"Just call me Jason," he replied. His jaw dropped slightly, becoming all gristly and stiff.

I didn't care. When you take in boarders, you have to make it clear that you're not their pal. You can help them out when they need it—write a character reference for a job, for example, or recommend a dentist—but they have to understand that you are the landlady, not their friend, and that on the first of the month, you expect to collect the rent. No exceptions. No leniency. Anyhow, I was old enough to be the mother of any of them. My son Ignacio was in his thirties already. Jason could damn well call me Mrs. Montez.

The following Sunday he came down for breakfast just as I was getting home from

Mass. I'm not Catholic, but sometimes I went with some of the boarders.

"Good morning, *Mrs. Montez*," he sniggered.

I usually didn't see him in the mornings. He had to be at the bakery at four in the morning, long before I'd left for my job at the bank.

"How are you, *Mrs. Montez?*" He had a pinched-faced grin, as though he carried a wad of bitters under his tongue.

I thought: Sorry it bothers you, son, but just suck it up. I didn't say it out loud, though. He was wearing a backward baseball cap, and I had the impression it was meant as a provocation. I overlooked it. I really didn't care what he wore except in my dining room at dinnertime.

I handed him the newspaper. "Want it?"

He took it from me, glanced at the headlines, and threw it back on the table.

"There's coffee in the pot," I added.

Corey Frater came into the kitchen and sat down at the table.

"Morning, Mrs. M," he said jovially.

Of all the young men to whom I'd rented rooms after Ignacio deployed, Corey was my favorite. He was from somewhere in the South—Georgia, I think—and his manners were from another era.

"I'm gonna get some coffee," he announced, getting up. "Can I get you something, ma'am?"

"You're *supposed* to call her *Mrs. Montez*," snapped Jason.

Corey stared at him as though he were a toad. Jason hesitated a moment, then turned and sauntered out the back door.

"We have to be patient with him," I said after an uneasy pause. "Maybe he's suffering from PTSD."

"Maybe he's just a... excuse me, ma'am... Maybe he's just a moron."

"Who knows what he went through over there, what he saw. Don't be harsh, Corey. Some of these young men suffered so much..."

"Pardon me for disagreeing," countered Corey. "We all saw a lot of bad stuff over there. There's no excuse for that kind of behavior. Listen, Mrs. M, if you make an omelet and it doesn't come out, what does that mean?"

"I guess it means you made a mistake."

"You can't make a mistake whipping up an omelet. If you make a bad omelet, it means you started out with bad eggs. Some of these guys were already nut cases when they went into the military."

"I think Jason's just immature. We have to be compassionate."

"Bah! He should have grown up by now. Anyhow, he didn't live through any horror stories in the Middle East."

"How do you know?"

"He was never in combat."

"He said he served in Iraq and Afghanistan!"

"In his dreams! He was in Kuwait three times. That's all."

"But why would he lie?"

"Some of these guys who weren't in the thick of it... they're embarrassed, they make up stories. But I know for sure that he was never there."

I must have looked flabbergasted because Corey laughed and said, "Recon, remember? I was in reconnaissance."

A couple of weeks later, Jason cornered me in the morning and told me he was planning to be home that evening for dinner. I didn't think to ask why he wasn't at the bakery already, but I don't remember that he looked as though anything were wrong. He'd never had dinner with us before because he usually got home from work in the late afternoon and went right to bed. Baker's hours—4 a.m. to 4 p.m.

"Okay, that's fine," I said. He was supposed to have let me know the day before, but I let it go. The stew was already bubbling in the Crock-Pot, and the kitchen was redolent with Moroccan spices, lamb, and garlic. I always made extra, so I knew there'd be enough. "See you tonight," I called as I ran out the door.

The air was leaden. A storm was brooding on the horizon like an angry giant. By noon the monster had begun to heave clouds like murky, wet, tattered blankets over the sky. Restless gusts battered roofs. The heavens growled. By early afternoon, drops like pitchforks were stabbing the lantana in the flower bed in front of the house. The trees shivered and begged for mercy.

Jason blew through the door about a half hour after the rest of us had begun eating.

"You were supposed to be here at seven," snapped Dan Lesko, a no-nonsense Marine as punctual as a German.

"Fuck you!" snarled Jason.

We all turned to stare at him. Corey shook his head in disgust.

"It's raining, in case you hadn't noticed, assholes! It's not so easy to get around on the buses."

"He means, 'Excuse me, ma'am. Sorry I'm late,'" said Corey, turning toward me. His distaste for Jason was palpable.

"I don't need you to tell her what I mean, asshole," snapped Jason. "I can speak! I have a mouth." He slouched down in his chair and ate his Moroccan stew without saying another word.

"It's delicious," said Dan. "Just terrific, Mrs. M."

"Absolutely terrific," Corey agreed.

After that, I noticed that Jason no longer left the house in the dead of night to get to the bakery at 4 a.m. or went to bed in the afternoon. However, he rarely joined us for dinner.

"Did you get another job?" I asked him one Sunday afternoon. I was mending some towels in the kitchen.

"You got your check on time this month, didn't you?"

"Yes, Jason," I said serenely. "I did."

His forehead was pale and lackluster under the visor of his baseball cap, but his eyes were feverish. He had the look of an impassioned martyr bracing for the arrows that would inevitably pierce his body. His gaze was steady. Defiant. The arrows would come, but he wouldn't wince.

"Something is the matter with that boy," I kept telling myself. "He has been through some trauma." But I didn't know exactly what it was or what to do about it.

It occurred to me that I should check his room. As a rule, I never entered my boarders' quarters. Each man was responsible for his own space and had his own key. I had a master, of course, but I didn't snoop. The men had use of the laundry room and washed their own clothes, changed their own sheets, and cleaned their own floors. I had no reason to invade anyone's privacy. And yet I was worried about Jason. What if he was on drugs? What if he had some serious medical condition? Or had lost his job? I knew nothing about his family. I couldn't get in touch with his mother. Did he even have a mother?

The next morning, I asked for an hour's leave at the bank and returned home at about 11:00. The house appeared to be empty. I tiptoed around and knocked at all the doors. I was especially cautious when I got to Jason's. I couldn't risk his catching me in the room. He might fly off the handle and do something rash.

I slipped the key into the lock. Adriana had loved lavender as a little girl, and my husband, Alejandro, and I had given in to her passion. Lavender walls with purple trim, lavender and pink flowered curtains, a lavender teddy bear, and an American Girl doll in a lavender nightgown. All that was gone now, of course. I had painted the room beige and brown when I started taking in boarders. Plain white venetian blinds. A utilitarian desk and chairs, with a sturdy dresser and bed.

Jason hadn't done much decorating. The walls were bare. No family photographs. In fact, no photographs at all. No computer. No books. No knickknacks. No military medals. I looked around for clues—a pill bottle, for example, or an alarming doodle on a notepad. Nothing.

I peeked into his closet. It was almost empty. A couple of pants thrown over hangers, two button-down shirts, a lone belt hanging on a belt rack.

I was loath to pull open his drawers, but I did. The first held a couple of crumpled T-shirts and a wad of money. Also a Swiss army knife with an exposed blade. The next one was empty except for one menacing object—a hard, black body like that of an overgrown cockroach or a horseshoe crab. It was a Glock 19. I knew because Alejandro had always kept a gun in the house for protection, and he'd had one just like it. After he died, I got rid of it.

I left the room. I wasn't sure what to do. I didn't want Jason to know I'd opened his drawer, but I also didn't want that gun in my house. I had told him the rules.

Back at work, I was nervous and distracted. I was afraid I was going to make a mistake with somebody's money. That evening, I waited until Corey returned home from the college, where he was taking courses in management, and pulled him aside.

"I can't be sure," I lied, "and don't ask me why I think this, but I suspect one of the men has a gun in his room."

Corey's answer took me aback. "It wouldn't surprise me," he said. "It's part of the culture. I'm sure every guy here owns a weapon."

I was speechless.

"Even me. But mine's out of reach, inaccessible. Anyway, don't worry about it. We all know the power of a firearm, and we're all trained in how to use one responsibly."

"But I *am* worried," I whispered. Did this mean that all of my boarders were flaunting the rules? I decided this wasn't the time to ask.

"You're concerned about Jason, right? I'll take care of it," Corey said coolly.

"You can't use your recon skills to sneak

into his room and steal his gun."

"I'll have a talk with him," Corey said. "Tomorrow I have an early class, but on Friday, I'll catch him before I go to school. He usually has breakfast at a little café by the college. He lost his job at the bakery, so he probably reads want ads on his iPhone and then goes out on interviews. I'm pretty sure he'll hand over his gun without an argument."

I felt better after that.

The next day, I was just pulling out of the driveway when I noticed Jason sitting on the steps in front of the house. I waved to him through the car window.

"Hey, Mrs. Montez," he called after me. I braked. He approached the car with his hands in his pockets, and even though I wasn't really afraid, I shuddered. "Listen, I'll be here for dinner tonight, okay?"

"Sure," I said, "fine. But in the future, please let me know the day before. We have rules, remember?" I tried to make myself sound as innocuous as possible.

Things went smoothly at the bank that morning, but in the afternoon there was a mix-up about a funds transfer from Abu Dhabi, which I finally had to get the central office to straighten out. I was bushed by the time I got home and was glad I'd left the coq-au-vin in the Crock-Pot in the morning.

Jason came into the dining room wearing an Orioles baseball cap and a torn T-shirt. He looked as though he'd just pulled himself out of bed. He sprawled onto the chair and sat hunched and wide-legged, staring at his rolls and butter as though they were very important. For a while no one said anything.

"Jason," I ventured finally, "I would appreciate it if you would please remove your cap. I'm a bit old-fashioned, I know, but I'd consider it a favor."

He straightened up and removed his cap. Another awkward silence.

"Great chicken, Mrs. M," Dan said finally.

"Yes, it is," added Corey.

The others echoed the compliment, and before long the incident had been forgotten. The subject had turned to the job market. There were openings in security and defense, if you wanted to go that route, someone was saying, but there was no real money in it. Better to go back to school and get a degree in business, said someone else. Morgan Stanley had jobs and so did Booz Allen. Was it better to pay a professional outfit to do your resumé or just do it yourself, Dan Lesko wanted to know. A while later, the conversation meandered over to football.

After dinner was over, I gathered up the dishes, then stuffed the garbage into a plastic bag to take out to the pail.

It was a clear, frosty night. With my free hand, I pulled my collar up around my ears. Leaves crackled underfoot. The low growl of the wind—something like the ron-ron of an anxious cat—muffled my footsteps. For an instant I thought I heard, or sensed, someone following me, but I looked around and saw only the shimmering pallor of the moon. I moved forward in the darkness toward the shed where I kept the trash. I could discern the silhouette in the moonlight. Suddenly I heard someone call. I turned. It was Jason.

"Mrs. Montez, I'd like to have a word with you."

"Of course, Jason."

I thought it was strange that he'd followed me outside to talk, but I wasn't frightened. I couldn't imagine that he would do something terrible right there in the yard.

"I want to tell you something." He was standing about two feet from me, and now I could see clearly that he was seething. He'd been nursing a low-grade rage for a while. But why? I'd tried to be fair, to overlook small irritations, and treat him with the same respect as everyone else.

"Listen, *Jacky*," he said with the same mocking tone I'd heard before, "you have no fucking business telling me what to wear. What I do and what I wear are... none... of... your... goddamn... fucking... business." He enunciated every syllable, spitting it out and into my face.

I had to bite my lip to keep from laughing. All this rage over a baseball cap?

"I'm not telling you what to wear, Jason," I said as sweetly as I could. "However, as I'm sure you know, it's considered disrespectful for a gentleman to wear a hat indoors in mixed company. Some people don't take those old rules very seriously anymore, but since you're going out into the professional world, and you never know what other people's sensitivities may be, it's a good idea to respect these social niceties to stay on the safe side. After all, why put yourself at a disadvantage? That's why I insist on the traditional rules of courtesy at dinnertime. Nothing personal."

Anyway, I thought, it's my house and I make the rules. But of course, I didn't say it.

He stood there, his eyes waxy in the moonlight. His whole being oozed loathing.

I turned and headed toward the shed. When I emerged, he was gone.

I was afraid I wouldn't be able to sleep

that night, so I took a couple of Advil PMs before I went to bed.

When I came down the next morning, Corey, Dan, and two or three others were huddled in the kitchen, murmuring.

"Did anyone get the newspaper?" I asked, suddenly nervous.

"Don't go out there," said Corey softly.

I looked from one to the other.

"It's Jason. We found him sprawled out on the lawn this morning, head blown to pieces, blood everywhere. He used his Glock."

"His baseball cap flew clear into the bushes," added Dan. "It's shredded."

I crumpled onto a chair. "We already called the police," said Corey.

"But I didn't mean to criticize him," I stammered. "I wasn't telling him what to wear. It's just that…"

"It's nothing you did, ma'am," said Corey, laying his strong, consoling hand on my shoulder. "The guy had a lot of problems."

I was sobbing disconsolately. "I didn't mean to hurt him," I kept repeating.

"Like I once told you, ma'am," said Corey, "when you get a lousy omelet, it's usually because you started with a lousy egg."

I shook my head. I felt as though I had a mouth full of dirt.

Sergeant Allen's Christmas

What threw me off was the way he kept laughing. He'd say a few words, then tilt his head back and guffaw, snorting and rasping like a cluster of rusty gears.

"A hell of a Christmas!" He had a Cheshire Cat grin that unnerved me.

"I saw on television where they have a big turkey dinner on the bases," I said. "They always show the soldiers gathered around a Christmas tree with some movie star beaming into the camera. Then they show the guys chowing down and wishing Merry Christmas to mom and dad or Aunt Gracie or…"

"Ain't nothin' like that, ma'am."

"That's what my son said."

Paul Allen had been living in my house for about three months. I almost hadn't accepted him as a lodger when he showed up at my door in answer to an ad. He'd struck me as slightly crazed.

"I'm fucked up," he said by way of introduction, "but not as fucked up as some of the other guys."

I stared at him in disbelief. Who did he

think he was, I wondered, using that kind of language? After all, he was a stranger in my home.

He was wearing a white T-shirt and jeans, with a baseball cap that said L.A. Dodgers. A shock of hair fell over his forehead, giving him a seductive air. I couldn't decide whether he was trying to look like a thug or a Latin lover.

"Could you please remove your cap?" I said coldly. "As a Marine, you should know…"

"Oh, hey, you know the rules," he said. "I like that."

I should throw him out, I thought, and I would have if it hadn't been for the stories.

"I was at Camp Blue Diamond in Ramadi," he began, as soon as he'd taken off his cap. "It was a fucking palace under Saddam, ma'am. I mean, a fucking palace with swimming pools, but hell, we weren't on no fucking vacation. We weren't jumping into no fucking swimming pool. I'm a sergeant now, but I went in as a private."

I tried to think of what to do. I certainly didn't want a nutcase living under my roof. On the other hand, he was clearly a talker. My own son never told me anything about what he'd experienced in Iraq. Whenever I'd ask him a question, he'd clam up. Pretty soon, I realized he just didn't want to talk about it. Who knows what he went through over there? I told myself. I knew he'd lost friends to snipers and roadside bombs. Certainly, he was in pain, but he made it clear his pain was private. I quit asking.

Yet I was insatiably curious about the war. I spent hours reading books and articles. I lay awake at night imagining Iraq. What did Ignacio feel when he patrolled those dangerous streets? What was it like when a ten-year-old pulled a knife on you? It occurred to me that Sergeant Allen would tell me things I wanted to know. It was worth the risk, I thought. But then, there was the question of his mouth. I had a "no swearing at the dinner table" policy in the house, although I didn't make an issue of it. After all, if you live with veterans, you can't be a prig. Most of them did tone down their language when they saw me coming, but some of them, like Paul Allen, just couldn't control it. In fact, they weren't even conscious of it. They said "fuck" every three words like some people say "like" or "you know," as in "I'm like going to the store to like buy some light bulbs because, you know, light bulbs are like on sale this week."

"All right," I told him. "Rent is due on the first of the month, and I need a month's deposit too."

"Sure, ma'am. You got a fucking nice house here, ma'am."

Paul Allen had a dirty mouth, but he was also as sweet as peaches. He worked as a security officer at one of the government buildings downtown—he knew how to handle a gun, of course—and arrived home early every afternoon, around 4:00. He'd set the table for me and my five or six boarders, then get out the greens and chop garlic for the salad dressing. I got home from the bank where I worked as a teller about 6:15. Before I'd even had time to change clothes, he'd start jabbering, and he'd keep it up while I made a salad, warmed the bread, and put together a dessert. I left the main dish in the Crock-Pot every morning. By evening, it was bubbling, and the fragrance of onions, spices, and wine-soaked beef filled the kitchen.

"There was this chaplain," he once told me as I made a pitcher of lemonade to put on the table. "What a fucking asshole. You can't imagine what assholes some of these guys are, ma'am. We had just lost a Marine, a seventeen-year-old private, and the guys are all ballin'. This moron comes in and says he's there to comfort us and make us understand that God had his secret ways. 'War is like a college football game,' he says. Can you imagine this, ma'am? The guys are all wrecks. The guy who died... the most loveable kid you could imagine. And this fucking son of a bitch says, 'War is like a fucking football game, a *college* football game.' We all wanted to deck the motherfucker. The lieutenant says to him—a cool guy, our lieutenant, Chavez was his name—Chavez says to him, 'War ain't like no football game, Chaplain. War is war. And anyhow, these kids ain't never been to college. They don't know what the fuck you're talking about.' I swear, ma'am. Some of these chaplains have their heads so far up their asses, they eat shit for breakfast, lunch, and dinner. Anyhow, the lieutenant got into a lot of trouble. The chaplain outranked him."

I smiled and sank into silence. I was thinking about the mother of the adorable seventeen-year-old.

Another time, I was grating cheese for enchiladas when he came into the kitchen. It was Saturday, so I was giving the Crock-Pot a rest.

"You know," he said, "once a guy came at me with a knife. I was on a raid, and this son of a bitch pops out of an alley with a blade the size of a bull's prick and stabs me in the shoulder. I spun around and kicked him in the balls. Then I pinned him against a wall until other Marines came and dragged him back to the base blindfolded, with his hands on top of his head. He gave me a good long slash. Wanna see?"

"No, Paul, not really."

"Here, Mrs. Montez. Look!" He yanked off his shirt and displayed a scar that seemed to slither over his upper back and across his shoulder like a hideous crimson and brown snake.

"Please, Paul," I said. "Put on your shirt. What if some of the guys come in! What will they think?"

He burst out laughing—that rusty-sounding guffaw that reminded me of gears. "They'll think Paul Allen is really hot stuff. Not even Mrs. M. can resist him!"

He put his arm around me and gave me a squeeze.

I smiled and didn't say anything. *Poor kid,* I thought. *He's lonely.*

On Sundays, Sergeant Allen got up early and went to the Eastern Orthodox Church downtown. He'd come home a few hours later with a bouquet of flowers, which he'd place in a vase. That would be the centerpiece for our table on Sundays.

The night he told me the Christmas story,

we were sitting in the kitchen drinking coffee. Within a couple of weeks, Paul would be going back to Los Angeles to spend the holidays with his family, and he was excited. His brother was married and had a little daughter, and his sister had just had a baby boy. Most of all, Paul couldn't wait to see his mom and dad. "You'd love my mom!" he told me. "She's a character!" We had to speak quietly. The other boarders had gone to bed or were studying in their rooms. Several had begun classes at the local university, but Sergeant Allen had no desire to go back to school.

"I was a lousy student," he told me. "My teachers told my parents I was smart but didn't apply myself. Me, I couldn't wait to graduate and enlist."

He poured a cup of decaf expresso for me and a cup of high-octane espresso for himself.

"I have the best memories of Christmas," he told me with a chortle. "It's my favorite holiday."

"Mine is Thanksgiving," I said. "That's when Ignacio and his sisters Adriana and Isabel come home to visit—at least, Ignacio comes when he's here on American soil. On Christmas, the girls go to their spouses' parents, but Thanksgiving is my day."

"I remember when I was little. We'd just come to this country…"

"You weren't born here?"

"We're Armenian. Allen is the name my parents took when they became citizens, but our real name is Avetisyan. This country gave us a chance, Mrs. M. After 9/11, I really wanted to go to war to defend America. That's the main reason I signed up. My mom cried the first time she saw me in uniform."

"I understand," I whispered, remembering the day Ignacio left for boot camp.

"Anyhow, when I was a kid, my mom would go out to the livestock auction and buy a lamb for Christmas. She couldn't bring it home on the bus, so she'd walk through the streets with the animal tethered with a rope!" He erupted into laughter. "Everybody would look at her like she was nuts, but she was fucking oblivious! That's what she did back in the old country, so she figured it was okay!"

He sat there chuckling for a while, then grew pensive.

"I remember one Christmas in Iraq," he said finally. "A hell of a Christmas." He started to laugh again. "I wasn't at Blue Diamond anymore. I was at a little base in the middle of nowhere. We'd put up a makeshift

Christmas tree—just some random bush—and decorated it with paper angels. I figured things would be calm. Even during World War II, they'd call a truce for Christmas. Shit, even the Muslims usually didn't attack on Christmas Day. It was kind of understood, you know." He smiled and shook his head. "The birthday of baby Jesus, it's sacred, for Christ's sake."

The guys were going about their business as though it were any other day, when the commanding officer called a bunch of us together.

"He looked right at me and started barking," said Paul. "'I need six volunteers. You, you, you, you, you, and you.' His finger was pointing right at my chest, like a pistol."

"He sent you on a mission on Christmas Day?"

"Yes, ma'am. I was *voluntold*; I didn't volunteer. By then, I was a corporal. I'd gotten a promotion because I was a good Marine, but I was still at the bottom of the totem pole. Anyhow, there was a hideout outside of Baghdad, he said, with an HVT. We had to get ready right away and leave during the night to get there before dawn."

"HVT?"

He guffawed. "Sorry, ma'am. 'High-value

target.' A big-shit Saddam operative. Remember the famous deck of cards? After the invasion in 2003, the American military put together a set of playing cards to help soldiers identify the most wanted bad guys in Saddam's government. This guy was number eight or ten, I can't remember. Maybe he was number thirteen. Anyhow, we had to get him and bring him in. The CO—sorry, Mrs. M, 'commanding officer'—said that we weren't supposed to kill the motherfucker unless we had to. What the fuck, I didn't want to kill the bastard. It was Christmas!"

He laughed so hard that he snorted.

"Want a glass of water?" I asked. He seemed to be losing control.

He stopped laughing and stared into space, that unhinged look in his eyes. I don't think he heard me.

"We received detailed instructions, packed the trucks, and took off in the middle of the night," said Paul, after a long pause. "We had some guys from EOD—fuck, ma'am, I mean 'explosive ordnance disposal'—just in case the place was booby-trapped. In fact, we had a whole explosives team with us—wild guys who wisecracked the whole time. The guy in charge was named Richard Sharma. 'Dick the Prick,' I called him. He had a hell of a lot a nose hair and a battalion of pimples on his chin. 'We're gonna fuck those little buggers to high hell,' he kept saying. 'We're gonna give those goddam towelheads a Christmas present that'll last 'em forever.' I thought it was a bad sign. 'Fuck, this sucks,' I said to myself. 'This guy is trigger-happy.' It also occurred to me that whole area could be mined, and the motherfucking target could be waiting for us with a bunch of goons. If that happened, they would open fire before we did. Or else Dick the Prick would shoot first, and they'd return fire and blow us to pieces. Either way, I would die. I was only nineteen at the time, and I had images in my head of my mother sobbing over my coffin. And there was this girl who worked at the Taco Bell. I'd always wanted to meet her, and now I never would. 'If I die in this fucking country, I don't want to die on Christmas,' I said to myself." Paul's shoulders were trembling with mirth. He roared as though he were remembering something hilarious.

Probably the whole thing was some kind of a Christmas joke, I thought. Probably when they got to the house where the bad guy was supposedly hiding, it would appear to be empty. The Marines would kick in the door and run inside to find a bunch of guys waiting for them with a tree and presents and maybe even a turkey dinner. As I said before, I was thrown off by his laughing.

The plan was to take the target by surprise, he explained. "We rolled along the road with no lights. We used night-vision goggles and the moon to guide us. We had to park a long way from the hideout and tiptoe through the filthy, garbage-strewn streets until we found the house. Everything had a ghoulish, greenish tint to it. Dick the Prick led the way. He was an asshole, but he knew where not to step. After all, the towelheads could've planted bombs. One of the explosives guys started singing 'Jingle Bells' under his breath. 'Shut up!' one of our guys hissed. The Prick giggled like a little girl."

"But it all turned out okay, right?" I whispered. I was still imagining them storming the house to find the commanding officer there, all dressed up as Santa Claus.

"Suddenly, the Prick said, 'Hey, wait a minute! Stop!' Fuck, I thought. Something's wrong. This is bad juju. He saw something. They're about to hurl a grenade. The Prick stopped walking and pulled out a block of C-4. 'What the fuck are you doing?' I whispered. C-4 is a fucking powerful explosive. It could level a hospital or a church. We sure as hell didn't need a whole block for this decrepit little shack, with its rickety door, rotting frame, and peeling paint. Besides, we weren't supposed to blow up the house. We were supposed to take the target alive. Crap, I thought. We'll all be reduced to blood and shit. 'Wait here,' said the Prick. 'I'll be right back.' He disappeared into the darkness."

"But Paul, you're here. You're okay. Nothing happened," I insisted. I was getting nervous.

"He was back in a minute or two. He was carrying a red ribbon he'd gotten from his team's radio operator, who was crouching behind a garbage heap about a hundred yards away. 'What's that for?' one of the guys asked him. 'You'll see,' he said."

I was beginning to get goose bumps. "Paul..."

"The Prick ties the ribbon around the block. 'After all,' he says, 'it's Christmas.' Oh, God, I thought. This is horrible. I was prepared to kick in the door and storm the shack, to pull the thug out of bed or to take care of the guards, but I wasn't prepared for this moron, Dick the Prick. There could be women and children in that shack, I kept thinking. Maybe the bad guy took kids to use as a shield, or maybe he actually lives there with his family. This bomb squad guy was risking lives unnecessarily. You have to understand, ma'am, that I was nineteen years old and a corporal. The Prick was ten years older than me and a staff sergeant. I couldn't say anything. 'I'll deliver his present,' he says. Then the idiot creeps out from the building we were hiding behind and makes his way over to the shack. We had our guns ready, but he made his way across the trash-strewn patch in front of the house without incident. At last, he got to the door. It must have taken him thirty seconds, but it seemed like a fucking hour. I'm holding my breath, ready to pee in my pants. The Prick isn't making any noise, but we can see him. When he gets to the shack, he turns around to look at us. He has this big grin across his face! He reaches up and attaches the block to the door, then darts back to cover. 'Wait a second!' I said out loud. 'We weren't supposed to kill the motherfucker unless we had to!' Staff Sergeant Dick Sharma turns to me and glares. I can see the whites of his eyes in the moonlight. 'Listen, boy,' he snarls. 'I want to get this over with. I don't want to spend the whole fucking night here. It's Christmas.'"

I gasped. I couldn't think of what to say. Paul was slumped over his coffee, both hands on the table, still laughing. "I guess there was no way to warn…" I began.

"One hell of a Christmas, just like I told you, ma'am," he interrupted. "As soon as Sharma got back, we took off back down the road toward the trucks. The explosion was so violent that it lit up the neighborhood. The Prick was still guffawing. He actually thought it was funny. The flames stretched up into the night sky until they reached the moon—all yellow and gold and white and burgundy. It was actually beautiful. It's hard to explain. I asked the Prick, 'Do you think anyone was in there with him?' 'If there was,' he barked, 'they ain't there now.' He started howling like a maniac. He was right. No one could have survived that blast. Some of Saddam's guys were probably inside that shack with the target, but like I said, he could have had women and children with him too." He paused. "Children," he whispered. "Innocent little children." He was trembling.

"You don't know that, Paul," I said softly. "Don't torture yourself."

He was still crumpled over the cup. "That's what we did for Christmas." He sighed and shook his head. "That's what we did to celebrate the birth of Jesus Christ, our Savior. We killed a guy. Maybe more than just one guy. Maybe a bunch of kids too."

He sat there, slumped over his coffee, his face in his hands. His body was convulsing with laughter, that gear-grinding laughter that made me cringe. Tears poured down his cheeks like rain running over rutted terrain.

His laughter had morphed into sobs. What I had taken for mirth had actually always been grief. The tough language and flippancy were a façade. He was like a grapefruit that looks firm and ripe and whole, but once you pierce its skin and drive the needle into the pulp, its bitter juices gush out. Paul Allen was a spigot of sorrow.

I reached out and held his wrist. Neither of us spoke.

Green Eyes

All you could see was her eyes, green as a fresh pasture, gleaming through the slit of her burka. Sergeant Lindgren tried not to look directly at her. The woman was obviously hostile — perhaps resentful, perhaps frightened, perhaps both. She knit her brow and contracted her eyes into a squint.

"Tell her we're here to help, Saddiq," Lindgren told the interpreter.

"She won't believe you," he answered. "Last time the Marines were in this village, they kicked in every single door and searched the houses. Maybe they took away her husband or her brother, for all you know."

Lindgren sighed. "Tell her it's different now."

Ever since the surge, the dramatic increase in troops that took effect in 2007, more and more Sunnis had been cooperating with the Americans. As a result, many neighborhoods in Ramadi and nearby villages were calmer than they had been in years. People were beginning to venture out to the markets, children played in the streets, schools were reopening. Still, there were pockets of resistance. Some locals still didn't trust the foreigners, and the woman with the green eyes was clearly suspicious.

"Tell her I'm female, just like she is," said Lindgren.

Then, turning toward her, Lindgren added, "I've brought some supplies. Water, rice, that sort of thing." She knew that the woman couldn't understand her, but she wanted her to hear her voice.

The burka-clad woman jerked her head like a skittish colt, then disappeared behind the drab door of her drab house. The whole village was a dull sand-color, which is probably why the Marines, with perverse irony, called it Hollywood.

"This is pointless," said Saddiq. "We should talk to the elders, but, of course, they won't deal with *you*."

They tried three more houses. Even though Sergeant Lindgren caught sight of shadows behind the curtains, no one answered.

Sunlight fell implacably on the dirt road from the motionless sky. It beat down on the soldiers' helmets, giving Christine Lindgren an excruciating headache. She wished she had an aspirin and a glass of iced coffee. She wiped the sweat from her temples with her sleeve.

"Isn't it unusual for an Iraqi to have eyes that color?" she asked Saddiq, as they walked toward the truck they'd left at the edge of the village.

"It's unusual, but not unheard of."

On the way, they met up with two other Marines. "Any luck?" asked Saddiq.

"None," said Corporal Wang. "Sergeant Lindgren, if you'd permit me to make a suggestion, I think we should try to meet with the women in groups. Trying to approach them one at a time isn't working at all."

"Sonya, you're welcome to make suggestions, but I don't know how we could pull it off. We'd have to find a female interpreter, and even if we did, it doesn't seem like these gals want to have anything to do with us."

"I think they're just scared. They still see us as the enemy, even though the men seem to be coming around. Could you mention it to Lieutenant Montez, at least?"

Lieutenant Montez listened to Christine Lindgren's report with his usual poker face, which is why his response surprised her.

"I've been thinking about this a while," he said finally. "We're not getting through to these women. We've tried talking to them individually. Now let's try something else." He paused and swallowed. "What we need is a female representative at the village council meetings. We need to know what's on the women's minds. They need to be able to express themselves freely to someone they trust, someone who's a friend… or a neighbor. Someone who can then tell us what their concerns are."

Wow, thought Christine, *and I thought Sonya's suggestion was radical!*

"With all due respect, Sir," she said, "there's never been a woman at one of those meetings. Not in all the thousands of years since the Garden of Eden."

"The thing is, women make up over half the population, and we have no idea what they're thinking. I bet I could convince the elders that this constitutes a security risk."

"Well, if anybody has the *wasta* to do it, you do, Sir." She used the Arabic word that means something between "connections" and "clout."

Montez smiled. "In the meantime, I want you and Saddiq to go back tomorrow. Take Wang with you."

Christine sighed and looked at the floor. "Yes, Sir," she said.

Collapsing onto the battered sofa in the

next room, Christine tried to shut out the drone of Montez's voice. Her head still throbbed. She felt as though a bell were clanging inside her brain. Montez was talking to one of his assistants, a sergeant named Pantelis, about medical equipment. Only twenty-four years old and with no hospital management experience, he'd been ordered to revive the local medical facility. Semi-dozing, she caught snippets and phrases: "dinars... clinic... shambles... surgical tables... unusable... short-age... stethoscopes, syringes, bandages..." And then, a complete sentence: "We're starting from scratch, Pantelis... We'll set up a makeshift medical center until we can make the hospital serviceable."

Christine got up and fetched a bottle of water, then sat down again to sip it. Her mind wandered to her little daughter, Eva, only two years old and already talking in sentences. Christine and her husband had deployed at almost the same time, he to Afghanistan, and she to Iraq. They'd left Eva with Christine's mother. Thank God for email, thought Christine. At least she could get photos of her baby regularly. Her attention suddenly snapped back to the conversation in the next room. Pantelis was clearly getting on

Montez's nerves.

"Why do we have broads here, Sir?" said the sergeant. "They can't fight and we're not allowed to fuck them."

"They can do all kinds of things that we can't," answered Montez drily.

"Like what?"

"Like talk to Iraqi women and find out what they're thinking."

"But we're not talking to them," whispered Christine.

Christine Lindgren and Sonya Wang returned to the village they called Hollywood a few more times, but the green-eyed woman remained hidden. They decided to wait until market day, hoping that now that things were calmer, she might dare to go out shopping. It's true that the stalls were still mostly empty, but after the months of violence, many Iraqis were anxious to get out of the house and visit the souk.

At last, they saw someone trudging down the road, a shopping bag on her arm, a small girl scampering behind. They couldn't be sure this was the green-eyed woman. She wore the same black burka as nearly every other woman in the village, and she kept her head bowed and her eyes lowered.

"*Salaam!*" called out Christine, as the

woman approached the house. Christine and Sonya bowed.

"Tell her I just want to ask her something," Christine told Saddiq. "And tell her that Corporal Wang and I are both women!"

Saddiq hurled the words at her just as she disappeared behind her door, dragging the child behind her.

"She's not going to cooperate," said Saddiq. "Let's try somewhere else. There will be plenty of women returning home from the souk."

The three of them stood there deliberating.

Suddenly, the door opened a crack. The green-eyed woman stared at Christine and Sonya, her gaze wandering from the helmet to the camouflage uniform to the heavy combat boots, and resting first on the gun and then, with an intensity that would have been rude back home in the States, on their breasts.

"They really are women?" she asked Saddiq.

He nodded.

"Tell them to take off their headgear."

"She wants you to take off your helmets," he said. "She wants to see your hair."

Christine knew she was breaking a rule by

removing an essential part of her uniform but decided that compliance with the request was essential to her mission. She pulled off the helmet to reveal a short, blond bob. Sonya did the same, exposing a tight black chignon at the nape of her neck. The woman stared at the two young Americans, as if trying to figure out how these lovely creatures, with their soft skin, girlish features, and modest hairdos could be soldiers. Her penetrating eyes were as green as the Garden of Eden must have been when its lush vegetation covered the Tigris and Euphrates Valley. Christine smiled, but the woman did not smile back.

"Ask her what her name is," said Christine.

Saddiq complied. "Her name is Rana," he said.

"Tell her she has beautiful eyes."

"That would not be appropriate."

"Tell her…"

Rana interrupted with some words in Arabic.

"She wants you to come into her house," said Saddiq. "This is an honor. She is beginning to trust you."

The women moved toward the door, but Rana held out her hand to indicate that Saddiq should stay outside. Christine shrugged, and she and Sonya followed Rana into the one-room house. A few mats on the floor for eating and sleeping, a shelf for cooking utensils, and a rickety table were the extent of the woman's possessions. The child they had seen earlier and two older girls who looked to be around ten and twelve years old hovered by the wall.

Rana went over to the table where the shopping bag lay and emptied it out onto the table. A few vegetables—eggplant, okra, courgettes, onions, and tomatoes—as well as small bag of barley constituted the entire contents. She pointed at her purchases and then at the children and lifted her hands in a gesture of despair. An avalanche of words followed. The Marines understood she was frantic over the lack of goods in the market.

Christine stuck her hand in her pocket and whipped out a photograph. "Look," she said.

The woman gaped at the image of the bouncy blond child, her lips parted in a giggle.

"Eva," said Christine. "My baby." She pantomimed a mother rocking her child.

The Iraqi woman opened her impossibly green eyes so wide they looked like enormous emeralds. "Eva," she whispered. She shook her head. She clearly didn't understand what Christine was doing in Iraq when she had a child back home. She looked at Sonya and raised her eyebrows.

"No," said Sonya. "No babies. Not yet."

They signaled for her to follow them outside.

"Tell her that we'll be back tomorrow with rice," Christine told Saddiq.

Rana and Saddiq spoke for longer than it would have taken the interpreter to relay the message.

"She says she cannot feed her family with what she can buy at the souk. She has five children—three daughters who stay home with her, and two sons who go to the cobbler's shop her husband owns with his brother."

Rana stood staring at the ground, bowed in desperation. Christine took some candy out of her pocket and gave it to the children, who huddled around their mother.

"She wants to know where your baby Eva is," Saddiq added.

"Tell her that she's at home in Grand Marais, Minnesota, with her grandma." Christine felt as though she had a wad of wool stuck in her throat.

The next day, the Marines returned with a large bag of rice. Rana signaled for the women to sit down on a mat, then brought a pot of tea and three cracked cups that had once been pretty. For the first time, she smiled at the two Americans.

Her gaze went from Christine to Sonya and back again. Finally, she pointed to Sonya's eyes and made a questioning gesture, with upward turned palms.

"Corporal Wang's family was originally from China," explained Christine, fully aware that Rana didn't understand a word she said. "Americans are from all different ethnic backgrounds. Corporal Wang is from San Francisco, where there is a large Chinese population."

Rana shook her head and smiled. Christine and Sonya both shrugged, as if to say, "That's just the way it is."

Christine pointed to their hostess' green eyes and made the same questioning gesture. Rana laughed and nodded to show she understood. Then she shrugged, as they had done. "That's just the way it is."

"We need a female interpreter," Christine told Lieutenant Montez when she returned to base. "We're making progress, but we need to be able to speak with Rana."

"I'm meeting with the elders this afternoon," said Montez. "It's a longshot, but I'm going to ask for a woman representative on the council. See if Saddiq can get Rana to meet with other women to find out what they need and to elect a spokesperson."

"A meeting of women," said Christine. "That's just what Sonya Wang suggested."

A week later, about thirty women from the neighborhood packed into Rana's tiny house. In their black burkas, screeching and squawking all at once, they reminded the Americans of a flock of blackbirds. In spite of the furious pecking and snapping, by the end of the afternoon, they had chosen an envoy named Marjani and made a list of three wants. Christine and Sonya were present at the gathering, and although they understood no Arabic, they knew from the smile on Rana's face that it had been a success.

Rana pushed Marjani toward them. The newly elected delegate wore a long, thin *abaya* over her dress and an *asha* over her hair, but her face—as beautiful and evocative as a poem—was bare.

"I, Marjani, speak for women," she said, grinning widely.

"You speak English!" exclaimed Christine and Sonya in unison.

"Little bit." She shook her head and lifted her hand, pinching her thumb and index finger almost together to show that her English was very limited.

The first council meeting that Marjani attended was something of a shock to the elders' systems. Montez had used all his *wasta* to convince the sheiks that their failure to consider the women's concerns could seriously undermine stabilization efforts.

"We need to integrate the women and get them on our side," he told them. "Otherwise, they could harbor resentments and work against us."

"This has never been done!" objected some.

But one old sheik, a heavy-faced man with the eyes of a seer, challenged his brothers. "The young American is right," he said. "Women can be treacherous, and there's no way to know what they've got in their heads. Give them a voice. It will avoid problems in the long run." Montez understood enough Arabic to chuckle at the reasoning of the eldest of the elders.

Marjani began to enumerate her neighbors' requests. The women needed some kind of public transportation, she explained, because they weren't allowed to drive and had no way to get their children to the doctor or wherever else they had to go. They also wanted a park, since it was now safe for youngsters to play outside. The council members nodded. So far, the women's wishes sounded reasonable. Montez said the Marines could organize a jitney service from Hollywood to Ramadi without much difficulty. Working with Iraqi engineers and laborers, they could also build a playground with swings and slides and other playground equipment. It was the third of the women's requests that left the sheiks dumbfounded. Marjani explained that the women wanted to work, to start their own small businesses, selling the products they made or grew. However, that required capital—for thread and yarn, for seeds and tools—that they didn't have. What the women really needed, Marjani explained, was cash.

The sheiks began to grumble. They were strapped for funds themselves, and they certainly were not going to lend the little money they had to a bunch of women who, in their opinion, should be at home tending their babies. "Women starting businesses! Whoever heard of such a thing?" groused several of the men. Montez remained silent, but when he got back to base, he turned on his computer and looked through his contact list. The year before, he had met a State Department representative who was knowledgeable about the Grameen Bank, which made collateral-free microloans to impoverished people anxious to start businesses. He wasn't sure how much *wasta* he had with the U.S. government, but that afternoon he shot off an email to Kelly-Lou Grotsky, explaining the situation in Hollywood, the little village on the outskirts of Ramadi.

To his amazement, she answered almost immediately. She had a colleague named Cynthia Lerner, she said, who was in Baghdad working on the reconstruction effort. Kelly-Lou was sure Cynthia could help. Montez was encouraged, although he knew the government bureaucracy was a lumbering animal, a cross between an elephant and a snail, and, he'd need the approval of the elders, in addition to help from the State Department.

Montez managed to assemble a fleet of jitneys to work the Hollywood-Ramadi corridor faster than he was able to secure a meeting with Cynthia Lerner. By the time she roared up to the gates of the base three months later in her Army-issued Jeep, the jitneys had been running for several weeks, and the sandlot designated by the elders for the children had been turned into a playground. It was, admittedly, like no playground any American had ever seen before. There was no grass, only sand—one massive sandbox surrounded by all-weather, rustproof jungle gyms, slides, swings, and monkey bars, as well as a playhouse with (and this was quite incredible) an aquarium. The sign on the gate, which the old sheik had made, said, "Lt. Ignacio Montez Playground" in English and Arabic.

Cynthia Lerner climbed out of the jeep and blinked the sand out of her eyes. Her red-blond hair glistened in the sunlight, and if Montez had bothered to think about it, he would have realized that she was pretty. However, Montez would be leaving Ramadi in eight weeks, and Marjani had made it clear that the women were still clamoring for stalls in the souk. His mission was to get them the microloans they needed, and there could be no distractions.

"I'll be a couple of hours," she said to the driver in Arabic. "Go have lunch."

"You speak the language!" exclaimed Montez. He could feel his spirits lifting, but he knew better than to put too much faith in a bureaucrat. He called for Christine and Sonya.

When the two Marines arrived at Rana's little house with Cynthia later that afternoon, they noticed something unusual. Instead of her usual black burka, Rana was wearing a long, flowing, turquoise *dishdasha* and a matching headscarf, both exquisitely embroidered with tiny yellow flowers. Her face was bare, and her dazzling green eyes glowed as she jabbered with her neighbors.

Cynthia introduced herself in Arabic. The women stared. Her bare head. Her spectacular ginger-colored hair. Her ruddy, freckled face. And her eyes, as bright and emerald as the Euphrates at sunrise. She smiled at Rana.

"We have the same color eyes," said Cynthia.

"Yes, we do," said Rana, beaming. "We are sisters!"

Cynthia listened and took notes. It was the first time any of them had met an Arabic-speaking Western woman or had a real conversation with an American.

"We can do it," Cynthia told Lieutenant Montez and Christine after she had met several times with the women she now called the Hollywood Stars. "It will take a while, but we can do it! These women are smart, energetic, and ambitious. I want to help them."

Montez took the news to the elders.

"Yes," said the old sheik. "Let them have their businesses. It will keep them busy and also bring money to their families."

Montez breathed a sigh of relief.

Two months later, while he and his men were preparing to turn the base over to the next division, word came that Cynthia Lerner had received approval for the microloans.

"Wow," said Pantelis. "The broads made it happen! I can't believe it."

"Told ya," growled Montez.

* * *

Ignacio Montez—now Captain Montez—sat down at his desk and turned on his computer. California sunlight streamed through the window and fell in patches all around him. The base was a beehive, as new platoons prepared to deploy. Montez poured himself a coffee and opened his emails. One caught his eye.

Dear Ignacio,

I hope you're readjusting to life in the States. No more tiptoeing through the streets, dodging roadside bombs!

I wanted you to know that I was back in Hollywood last week and visited Rana at her shop in the souk. She had an unbelievable assortment of kaftans and scarves that she designed, sewed, and embroidered herself, and now that the economy is picking up, she is beginning to sell them. She gave me a lovely purple scarf, which I will send to Christine when I get home. After all, she's the one who really made this happen. Rana and Marjani send their regards. Whenever I mention your name, they say, "Now there's a man with *wasta*!"

Best regards,

Cindy

The Chaplain

On the afternoon Captain Guthrie appeared on my doorstep, I was wearing a bathing suit and a beach wrap. It was embarrassing. After all, I'm not a young woman, and I don't have the figure of a teenager.

It was a sultry afternoon in July, one of those muggy summer days that make your clothes stick to your body like a membrane. The men were all out, so I'd slipped into my grungy old swimsuit and had been down on all fours scrubbing the kitchen floor when the bell rang.

"I wasn't expecting you so early," I said, rag in hand. "Sorry I'm such a mess."

Captain Guthrie smiled. "Don't worry about it."

I'd been taking in veterans since my son Ignacio left for Ramadi in 2005. One veteran brought in another, and soon I'd rented every possible space in the house. When summer evenings were cool, we sometimes barbecued in the backyard, but most of the time, I'd get busy in the kitchen right after work, and soon the spicy fragrance of freshly baked empanadas and *pastel de choclo* or hearty beef stew filled the house. I began to look forward to dinnertime. I'd set the table with flowered dishes and colored tumblers. I'd decorate with gourds in the fall and poinsettias at Christmastime. I wanted to make it nice for them.

The men sat around the table and ate with gusto. They'd had their fill of MREs and welcomed a home-cooked meal. I loved hearing their fierce opinions about football and politics, but also the chitchat, the laughing, and the teasing. I had a "no-swearing within earshot of Mrs. Montez" rule, which most of them respected most of the time. They never talked about war at the table, but sometimes, one of them would wander into the kitchen late at night and tell me stories over a cup of coffee. Having vets around made life more bearable.

Captain Guthrie was a different kind of boarder. Identified only as M. L. Guthrie on the application, all I knew was that the candidate was an Army chaplain with a master's degree in Religious Studies and plans to pursue a degree in counseling at the local university. Even though I knew from experience that names don't always tell you much about a person, I imagined a hefty Irishman with a blond buzzcut. The person who appeared on my doorstep was a pert young woman in her late thirties with an easy smile and eyes that reminded me of pools of chocolate. She was dark-complected and small-framed, but muscular. She looked like she could hold her own in a fight. On her left cheek, she had a burn scar the shape and size of a maple leaf, burgundy-colored and shiny, like polished leather, with a spider web of blood-red capillaries running through the center of it.

"Bet you were expecting a big Irish sourpuss," she said by way of greeting.

I burst out laughing. "What are you, a mind reader? You must be Captain Guthrie, the Army chaplain."

"And you must be Mrs. Montez, the Marine mom who rents out rooms to vets."

"Jacqueline Montez," I said, holding out my hand.

"Margarita Luisa Guthrie. People are always surprised when they meet me. You can call me Meg. What should I call you?"

"I prefer Mrs. Montez," I said, tugging at the wrap to cover more of me. "Now that you've seen all my bulges and bruises, I have to assert my authority somehow!"

She grinned. "Montez sounds Spanish."

"So does Margarita Luisa."

"My mother is Mexican. My father was a lay instructor at the Jesuit college in Guadalajara. I grew up there. *¿Habla español?*"

"Not very well. I was born in Chile, but my family left when I was about twelve."

"I'm rusty, too. I haven't spoken Spanish in years. We spoke mostly English at home, and I moved back to the States when I was a teenager. Before they meet me, people always assume I'm a ruddy blonde. Afterwards, they don't know what to think. I always have a lot of explaining to do. But to tell the truth, you don't look like my idea of a Montez. I mean, you're so blonde and fair..."

"People make all sorts of assumptions about Latin Americans, but Chile is largely European. I'm a Sephardic Jew. Montez is my husband's name—he passed away five years ago. My family name is Jaén, but here they pronounce it 'Jane' instead of 'Ha-en,' so I use Montez. It's easier."

"Wow, jumping to conclusions like that... I should know better."

I laughed. "Happens all the time, Meg," I said. "You never really know what the other guy's story is. Here, let me show you your room."

Meg was my second female boarder. The first was Sandra, whom the Army had yanked out of her medical program and deployed to Afghanistan before the end of the semester. I felt an instant connection with Meg, just as I had with Sandra. I loved my male boarders, but Meg was special. When I got home from work, she'd have set the table. Often, we'd spend hours in the kitchen comparing recipes. She fried empanadas—those succulent meat pastries ubiquitous in Latin America—and I baked them. She made *carne guisada* (stew) with beef, chili and cumin. I made *cazuela* with meat and chicken.

I had a gas range, and I noticed she was squeamish about fire. She'd stick things in the electric oven, but when it came to placing pots on the burner, she'd hang back a moment to see if I'd take care of it. If I didn't, she'd take a breath and approach the flame, but I could tell she felt uncomfortable, so I tried to deal with the stove myself. On the nights we barbecued, she'd stay in the kitchen making a salad until one of the guys—usually Corey or John—got a flame going. I figured it might have something to do with her scar, but I never asked. I'd learned early on that when dealing with vets, it's better not to ask questions. You never know what ugly memories you might conjure up.

When I made *a bistec a lo pobre* or a *palta reina*, I'd sometimes become melancholy.

"This is one of Ignacio's favorite dishes," I whispered one evening, blinking back tears.

"God is watching over him, Mrs. Montez. Would it help if we prayed together?"

"I don't pray. I just want my son to come back safe and whole from this damned war." She placed her hand on my wrist and squeezed gently.

After dinner, we'd sometimes watch a movie together or sit in the kitchen drinking tea or coffee.

"You know," she said one evening when we were relaxing on the porch, "prayer really can be helpful—even if you don't exactly believe... well... completely. Whenever we had a risky mission ahead of us, the guys would form a circle and just observe a few moments of silence. I'm sure some of them prayed, but not all of them. A sergeant named Ken told me he was an atheist, but even so, those circles helped calm his nerves. He was the sweetest kid, so kind to everyone, even the Al-Qaida we dragged in. He adopted a couple of stray dogs, and we all helped him hide them from the commanding officer. 'I don't know,' he told me, 'I just don't believe in God.'

'It doesn't matter,' I said. 'God believes in you.'"

I smiled. I imagined Ignacio saying something like that and then smirking when he heard her answer. "Sometimes, when I was a child, I'd hear my father chanting," I told her. "*Sh'ma Yis-ra-eil, A-do-nai E-lo-hei-nu, A-do-nai E-chad*. It was beautiful." I paused and remembered my father, his prayer shawl wrapped over his shoulders, chanting and swaying back and forth rhythmically. "We belonged to a Sephardic synagogue in Valparaíso," I went on, "but here, I pretty much lost contact with the community. And now, with the boarders, I do what I can to make them feel at home—bacon and eggs, Christmas decorations—that sort of thing."

"My mother taught me the rosary. *Dios te salve, María. Llena eres de gracia: El Señor es contigo. Bendita tú eres entre todas las mujeres. Y bendito es el fruto de tu vientre: Jesús*. I had to serve soldiers of all faiths, so I only said it when someone asked, but I repeated it to myself over and over whenever I felt afraid."

"And were you afraid often?"

"I had every reason to be. IEDs were everywhere. Once one of our conveys rolled over a bump in the road outside of Nasiriya. Boom! The flames were so high and so intense, you felt as though your body were melting off your bones." Instinctively, she brought her hand to her cheek.

"Is that where...?"

"The first two trucks were in flames. We lost four men. The medics had set up a large tent about two klicks from there. They arrived almost immediately and started pulling guys out of the fire. They were applying first aid even before they got the wounded into the helicopter. I ran in and helped drag men to safety. *Líbranos del mal*, I prayed. *Deliver us from evil.*

"Yes," Meg said softly, "that's where I got this burn. Before I knew it, I was being evacuated myself, and you know what I was thinking, Mrs. Montez? I thought, boy, am I useless. The medics were trying to save lives, and me, all I could do was pray!"

"But you were also helping to get the men out of danger."

"You should have seen how those medics worked, applying tourniquets, compresses, salves. Bandaging up limbs." Her eyelids were moist. "And then they were attending to me, to *me*, when they should have been taking care of the wounded fighters."

She fell silent.

"I thought, these men don't need God and

they don't need me. They need painkillers."

She was dabbing her eyes on her sleeve.

"It wasn't until the next day, when I was bandaged up and back on the job, that I realized that I did have a role, that prayer was what a lot of them needed after all."

She went silent. I sat with her a moment longer, but she was lost in her thoughts, so I got up and went into another room.

* * *

Our routine changed when classes began in September. Meg was planning to become a rehabilitation counselor. She was studying on the G.I. Bill, and had a limited time to complete her degree, so she had taken a full load—The Psychology of Trauma, Medical Ethics, and Pacifism, a course taught in the Philosophy Department by Dr. Donald Thurston. Meg Googled him. "He's a smart guy," she told me. "A renowned anti-war activist. I'm sure we'll have a lot to talk about. I'm psyched!"

Oh no, I thought. Not Thurston. Thurston hated the military. Sandra had taken a course with him, and he had given her a hard time. If the Army hadn't pulled her out of school and sent her to Afghanistan, she might have failed his course and had to give up her dream of becoming a doctor. Fortunately, after completing her tour, she was able to recommence her studies at Columbia University and graduated with flying colors. I flew up to New York to attend her graduation. But would Meg be as lucky? I wondered. Or would Thurston wear her down until she dropped out of her program? Maybe he had a change of heart, I thought. Maybe he's stopped harassing veterans. But I was nervous.

"The ethics of war is a topic of great interest to me," she was saying, "and I'd love to hear the pacifist's perspective. As I said, I'm sure we'll have some great discussions."

But when Meg returned from her first class, she was less certain.

"He began with a question," she said. "'What do Albert Einstein, John Lennon, and Mahatma Gandhi have in common?' Of course, there's always some guy who knows all the answers. 'They're all pacifists?' the bright-eyed kid sitting next to me piped up. I must have smirked or scowled or something because Professor Thurston turned to me and frowned. I didn't think it was a big deal, though, because a few seconds later, he went on with his lecture." Meg stopped and looked at me before continuing.

"At first, he droned on and on about the meaning of pacifism: the absolute opposition to violence in all its forms. 'A real pacifist refuses to pay taxes, since the state is the perpetrator of war,' he proclaimed. 'Of course, I do pay taxes. It avoids hassles with the government.' A couple of students chuckled, and Thurston looked pleased with himself. But the more he talked, the more agitated he got," explained Meg. "He was turning the color of a persimmon. He evoked everyone from Uchimura Kanzō to Joan Baez. By the end of the class, drops of sweat were splattering on his desk. For a pacifist, he seemed strangely fierce!

"I raised my hand and asked, 'What if a nation is attacked? What if a tyrant as evil as Saddam or Hitler begins torturing citizens? Doesn't the world have a duty to intervene? But he just shrugged. 'That's a sophomoric question,' he said. 'The same question kids like you always ask. Violence begets violence. Even if in the short run you save a few thousand lives, in the long run, you lose many more.' He hurried out of the room without giving me time to respond."

"Sounds like a bully," I said. "And what's this business about 'kids like you'? Damned patronizing!"

But Meg just shrugged and changed the subject. "I feel like cooking," she said. "What about if I make a *pastel de tres leches* for dessert?"

* * *

Fall was settling in. A misty drizzle coated the leaves. Clusters of red, orange, magenta and yellow gave the trees in my front yard a festive look. Soon I would be getting up early on Saturday mornings to rake and clear, but for now, I was enjoying the hues of the season. And the scents—pine needles, chrysanthemums, pumpkin pie spice, cornbread, sweaty socks left on the floor after football practice.

I slipped on my rain jacket and went out to the porch to wait for Meg, who usually came back from the university around four.

"I caught Professor Thurston before class today," she called as she strode up the steps. "I wanted to have a conversation with him. 'I hate war as much as you do,' I began. 'I've seen it first-hand. I was a captain in the Army.'"

"That must have taken him by surprise."

"He glared at me. 'I doubt you hate war as much as I do,' he said. 'In an all-volunteer army, people are there only because they want to fight.' I looked him straight in the eye and said, 'I've never met a man or woman who's actually experienced war who wants to fight. It's because I've seen war that I want peace. That's why I'm taking this course.'"

"That should have calmed him down. Maybe you'll develop a real friendship with Thurston."

"I doubt it. He just stood there glaring at me. 'You're taking this course because it's required,' he snarled. I didn't answer him. After all, it's true. If his course weren't obligatory, I'd drop it. I'm interested in intellectual give-and-take, but Thurston clearly isn't. 'How many innocent children did you kill?' he said suddenly. 'I didn't kill anyone,' I whispered. 'I was a chaplain.' I admit I was shaken. He burst out laughing. 'I suppose you told all those little morons that their cause was destined for victory because God was on their side.' I couldn't believe it, Mrs. Montez. Why such venom? I was trying to have a conversation, not an argument."

We went indoors. I'd bought some avocados a few days ago, and they were beginning to turn mushy. Meg spied them.

"I'm going to make guacamole," she said. "I feel like mashing something."

"Good idea." I paused a moment and then

started quartering limes. "But listen, Meg, you have to get through the course, so it might be more expedient to grin and bear it than to try to have a meaningful conversation with Thurston."

"He just kept growling at me," she went on. "'What does an Army chaplain do anyway? These kids can pray all they want. It's not going to prevent their heads from getting blown off.'

"'God doesn't prevent bad things from happening,' I told him, 'but faith gives us the strength to deal with evil when it occurs. God doesn't create wickedness. People do, or sometimes harmful situations occur because of natural phenomena. Earthquakes, that sort of thing. In times of crisis, people sometimes need spiritual support. That's where the chaplain comes in.'"

"What did he say?" I asked her.

"He said, 'Bullshit! No guy has spiritual needs when he thinks his balls have just been blown off. You think you're a spiritual guide? You're part of the problem! You're a gear in this military machine. You justify your part in the war by injecting religion into this whole rotten mess! You think you're so damned virtuous because you convince young men that killing is not a sin as long as they do it for

God and country! Well, guess what? Al-Qaida fighters have been sold that same bill of goods. They think it's okay to kill Americans because they're doing it for Allah!'"

I squeezed some limes into the mashed avocado. Meg stared at a pair of onions with an intensity I had never seen in her eyes before. Then she started chopping—*chop chop chop*.

"Later that afternoon, in class, he started in again," she said. "'You never had any doubts about what you were doing in the military, did you, Captain Guthrie.' It wasn't a question. He spat out the word *Captain* as though it tasted like dung. 'Many, many doubts,' I answered. He turned away from me and started talking about Buddhist pacifists. The other students were getting jittery. Some of them eyed me with curiosity, and some with irritation.

"But I was pissed. 'You know,' I said, 'most of the kids in this class have never been to war. I have. In a battle, you don't demoralize soldiers by talking about sin. You try to help them find spiritual strength in times of danger. I know what stress can do to a soldier. One time...' 'We're not interested in your war stories!' thundered Professor Thurston. 'How dare you interrupt my lecture!' But then one of the students blurted out, 'I am! I'm interested in her stories!' 'Yeah,' said someone else. 'Let her talk!'"

"I admire your gutsiness," I told her. "Did he let you go on?"

"That only enraged him more," she said. "He walked over to my desk and stood right in front of me. 'You think you're the only one here who's been in a war zone?' He was screaming now. 'You think you're the only one who's seen death? I lost my...' He caught his breath. Everyone was staring at him. Suddenly, he clammed up. He took a deep breath and pursed his lips. 'Please be quiet,' he said finally. He turned and stared at me. I recognized that look. I'd seen that pain in the eyes of too many soldiers. I looked down and stared at my book."

I hardly saw Meg for the next couple of days. She was studying hard, staying in the library until late at night. She had to pass every course in order to keep her G.I. Bill funding, and for that to happen, she had to avoid irritating Thurston.

One evening, we were sitting in front of the TV, sipping wine and not really watching. "How's it going with the Pacifism course?" I asked cautiously.

"It's a lost cause," she said with a sigh.

"I've got an essay due next week. The topic is Peace and War."

"That should be fairly easy for you," I said.

"Except that he wants me out of the program. No matter what I write, he's going to fail me."

I knew she was right. I remembered how he had attacked Sandra's essay years before. I really didn't know what to say.

"Write a really good argument, Meg. You'll see. He'll change his mind. Do you really think that deep in his heart he doesn't appreciate what you've done to help our soldiers?" I tried to sound convincing.

Meg thought about her essay for a long time, just as Sandra had. Maybe this time, I thought, he'll be more reasonable. After all, people change. But I wasn't optimistic.

Meg read about everyone from the Chinese activist Liu Xiaobo to the Berrigan brothers. In the end, she wrote about the IED incident she'd told me about. She showed the essay to me before she handed it in: "We were in the medical tent a couple of klicks from Nasiriya. It was a huge tent, latest equipment, even air conditioning. They'd sent in about fifteen doctors and a bunch of medivacs, but still, IEDs always catch you by surprise. It was horrible. There was nothing I could do but pull men out of the rubble."

He's not going to like this, I thought as I read through the paper. It's all about war, nothing about peace. But I didn't say anything. I read on:

"I felt useless. At a time like that, you don't think about politics. You don't think about morality. You think about the parents of these kids, what they're going to feel like when they find out they've lost a child. You think about the survivors, how they're going to get through this psychologically. They've lost limbs. Worse yet, they've lost buddies. To be honest, I really didn't know what to do. As soon as I was able, I met with each one of them individually—each one who wanted to talk to me—and we prayed together, and we cried. They needed a safe space, a space to cry. Yes, I talked to them about God, about the Cross if they were Christian, about how injustice and suffering are part of life. But this wasn't about Christianity or any other religion. It was about helping them find some sort of inner peace in the midst of the horror of war. I wasn't their commanding officer. With me, they didn't have to be strong, stoic soldiers. They could just let go. They could weep. That was my role as chaplain: to give them permission to weep."

I could feel the passion in Meg's words. She hadn't even mentioned her own injuries. That's what he's afraid of, I thought. Her passion. Her commitment, not to an ideology, but to other human beings.

As I'd feared, Thurston was furious.

"That wasn't the topic!" he barked at her in front of the whole class.

"Finding peace in your heart amid the savagery, Sir..."

"Thou shalt not kill, Chaplain. It's the sixth commandment. You should know that."

"A time to love, and a time to hate; a time for war, and a time for peace. Ecclesiastes 3:8. That's what I know."

I was proud of her. She'd stood up to him. She'd fought him with his own weapon: words from Scripture. But I was worried. Men like Thurston didn't like to lose, and she'd embarrassed him.

"What do you think he'll do now?" I asked her. She shook her head and said nothing.

* * *

Before I knew it, the semester was winding down. Most of my boarders were making plans for Christmas. I'd already begun pulling out the boxes of ornaments and tinsel. I was looking forward to the scent of pine needles and eggnog, bayberry and cinnamon.

One afternoon, I eyed Meg sitting in a corner looking dejected. Oh no, I thought.

"Thurston?" I asked.

"Yeah. He said my work had been shoddy all semester and there was no way I could pass."

"Meg, you have to file a complaint against this man. This just isn't fair."

"I don't want problems, Mrs. M," she whispered.

You have problems, whether you want them or not, I thought, but I didn't say it out loud. "Do you feel like praying?" I said finally. My own words surprised me.

"Not really."

I sighed. "Go see him in his office," I coaxed. "Up in front of the class, he has to play the tough, uncompromising idealist. After all, he has a reputation to uphold. But sometimes even a brute will soften when you talk to him one-on-one. Don't be confrontational. Just explain that you're an idealist, too. You want to help wounded veterans transition to a new life. You want to help people, just as he does. That's why you're studying to become a rehabilitation counselor. Does he even know what your career goals are?" She was weeping softly, and I handed her a tissue.

She shook her head. "It won't do any good," she hiccupped. "He won't listen."

"Then what are you going to do?" I asked.

She shook her head. "I honestly don't know. For now, I'm going help you get dinner. What are you making?"

"*Enchiladas mexicanas*, especially for you." She smiled weakly. "But there's no rush, Meg. Take your time. Go freshen up."

She disappeared into her room. A few minutes later I heard her murmuring: "*Salve María. Llena eres de gracia...*"

I remembered my own father chanting the *Sh'ma Yis-ra-eil* and felt calmer.

She came into the kitchen about a half hour later. "You know," she said, "I took your advice and prayed over it. I just didn't couldn't think clearly, so I asked God for guidance."

"And what did God tell you to do?"

"He told me to go see the dean."

"Good advice," I said. "I'm glad God and I see eye-to-eye on this."

The next morning, Meg trudged over the icy path to the dean's office. As I took deposits and handed out cash at the bank, I imagined her marching up the stairs to the Lloyd Building, confronting a bear-like secretary, and demanding to see the dean, only to be told he was at a meeting. She'd promised to call me after she'd spoken to him, and I left my cell phone on, against bank regulations. By noon, she still hadn't called, and I was beginning to worry.

I was counting cash when I suddenly looked up to see Meg standing in front of me. She wasn't smiling, but she didn't look crestfallen either. I caught my breath.

"Well?" I said. "Did you see the dean?"

"I did," she said. "She was very nice. She's a Navy veteran herself, so she understood the problem."

"And she's going to send Thurston to hell?"

"Unfortunately, you can't send a tenured professor to hell. He's got to stay at the university and make life hell for everyone else." Meg paused a moment, then added, "She said the course is required for the counseling program, so I can't drop it and stay in the program."

I looked at her in disbelief. "Does this mean…?"

Finally, Meg let me see the smile she'd been holding back. "She's going to let me change programs. There's one in psychological services that will allow me to pursue a career in counseling. The dean said the Army wouldn't have an objection, as long as I received credit for my other courses."

"And Thurston's class isn't a requirement?"

"No, not for this new program. Not only that, she's going to let me drop Thurston's class, even though it's officially too late in the semester to withdraw." She lowered her voice. "As a special favor. Because she understands."

I ran out into the bank lobby and hugged her.

"Thank God," I whispered.

"Thank God!"

"You see," she said that evening, as we prepared vegetables for dinner, "that's the power of prayer. God doesn't step in and solve your problems, but He does help you see things more clearly."

Mom and Dad

I noticed that he limped, but I didn't say anything. I've rented enough rooms to injured veterans to know that you should never ask them how they were hurt. Sometimes they'll bring it up themselves, but sometimes they don't want to talk about it. Mentioning it can conjure up bad memories. Best just to be quiet. Let them tell you how it happened if they want to.

Jeremy was one of the talkative ones. He opened up right away.

"Sniper fire!" he told me as he dragged in his suitcase. "Outside of Samarra. Just about shattered my hip. Didn't think I was going to make it."

He grinned widely, his black hair falling over his brow. His skin reminded me of soft Italian leather, and his eyes, of a waning gibbous moon.

"Lots of bad guys over there, ma'am. We got rid of a bunch of them. I was in recon. Snuck in behind their lines to find out what they were up to, and then, if we had to, we let them have it."

"I'm sorry… I'm sorry you were hurt," I stammered. I couldn't think of what to say.

"Mom and Dad went to see me in Landstuhl. Flew across the ocean just to see their little Jeremy. Amazing, right? I was in terrible shape. Gave them a hell of a scare. Landstuhl is the big Army medical facility in Germany, where they treat soldiers wounded in Iraq and Afghanistan."

"Yes, I know…"

"Afterward, the Army sent me to Walter Reed Medical Center, here in Maryland. That's how I wound up on the East Coast. Mom and Dad drove all the way from Cleveland every weekend to see me! Some guys don't have families, but me, I'm lucky. That's why I recovered so quickly. Listen, Mrs. M., I really appreciate your renting me this room. I love that it's near a university, so I'll be able to take classes at night. I want to study accounting."

"Are you in pain?"

"Huh?"

"Your hip. Does it bother you?"

"Oh, that. Yeah, sometimes. It used to hurt a lot, but now it's not so bad. Anyway, it's not bad enough to keep me from getting on with my life!"

"Good!" I smiled.

"I want to be an accountant like my dad. I got a job doing the books for a hardware store during the day, so you won't have to worry about the rent. I can pay it."

He was so typical of the vets who came to board with me, I thought. Stiff upper lip. No whining. Make the best of things. A lot of them had suffered injuries, physical or emotional. They'd lost legs. They'd lost buddies, saw children bleed to death. But whatever nightmares they had, they didn't share them, at least not with me.

"I'm not worried about the rent, Jeremy. These are your digs," I said, showing him his room. "Here's the key. You can keep it locked. I have a master key, of course, but I never go into the boarders' rooms unless there's an emergency repair to be made or something like that. Oh, one more thing… I told you over the phone that I recently got a cat, Petunia. I just want to make sure you don't have allergies."

"No worries about Petunia. I love animals. And you can come into my room whenever you want, Mrs. M. I ain't gonna hang no naked ladies on the wall." He winked and laughed. "Just pictures of Mom and Dad. Come on, look!"

He pulled a bunch of photos out of his

satchel and threw them on the bed. Mom and Dad on either side of Jeremy, on crutches, at Walter Reed. Mom and Dad standing by a Christmas tree. Mom and Dad surrounded by palm trees in front of what appeared to be a hotel.

"That one was taken in Hawaii," said Jeremy. "I bought them tickets to Honolulu. Mom had always wanted to go. I saved up my money while I was in Iraq." He picked up the photo and stared at it. Then his smile abruptly faded, and I thought that maybe his hip was hurting him.

"A lovely couple," I said to break the silence. They were, too. Mom, reedy and graceful in her body-hugging skinny jeans. Dad, muscular and athletic. Mom looked like a teenager, although I calculated that she must be in her fifties. She had curly auburn hair that hung seductively over her shoulders. Dad had long, straight hair, black as liquorish and tied back in a ponytail.

"Dad isn't really an accountant," said Jeremy suddenly. "I mean, he's the business manager of a company… but he doesn't have a degree in accounting."

I didn't know quite what to say. "It doesn't matter to me," I mumbled after an awkward silence. "What kind of business?"

"He's in construction," said Jeremy quietly.

"Oh, my husband was in construction," I said, although it wasn't quite true. My husband had been an architect, and that seemed close enough. The important thing, I thought, was to create a bond with Jeremy, to make him feel that we had something in common. It's not that he was alone—after all, he had his mom and dad—but he seemed... I don't know... vulnerable.

Jeremy picked up his suitcase and threw it on the bed. He turned to me, his smile once again broad and bright. His perfect teeth made me think of an advertisement for Colgate.

"Yes, a lovely couple," he echoed. "Mom is from Montana. Dad is from San Francisco, but his parents were born in the Philippines."

"Where did they meet?"

"In a coffee shop in San Francisco. My mom was working there. But then they moved to Ohio because Dad got a job in Cleveland."

I didn't ask what kind of a job it was. His bearing had changed again. His shoulders had stooped in what seemed to be resignation, and his expression had become pained. The hip, I thought.

He caught me staring at him and

suddenly wrenched himself up. His countenance brightened, and he flashed me that breathtaking Colgate smile.

"Do you need some aspirin or anything?" I asked on my way out.

He looked at me in mock puzzlement. "Aspirin?" he said with a grin. "Why would I need aspirin?"

It was early summer. Roses filled my garden, dainty herbal princesses in smooth, silk, blushing pink bodices. Their scent swept over me as I relaxed on the backyard swing and read the paper before going in to prepare dinner. Lilacs formed a chandelier over my head. Fleecy clouds fluttered like angels in paradise. On those sultry summer afternoons, sometimes one of the boarders would come home early and keep me company, but often I read or dozed alone, happy to have a few moments to myself. I had recently been promoted to assistant manager at the bank where I worked, and I appreciated this time away from the bustle and drama of complaining customers and a perpetually irritable boss.

That afternoon, I was still lounging in the garden, squinting at a particularly spectacular rose, when Jeremy walked through the gate. He was hardly limping at all.

"Look at that flower," I said as he sat down next to me on the swing. "It's the reddest rose in the garden. The color is so deep and intense that it's almost magenta. And look at those petals. So delicate, they remind me of lace."

"Like a young girl in a frilly, festive ball gown in a crowd of dowdy old women."

"What a lovely way to put it, Jeremy. So poetic and sensitive."

He blushed and began to fidget with his book bag. "Mom and Dad always said I was creative," he mumbled.

Dinner was bubbling in the Crock-Pot. I glanced at my watch. I still had a few minutes to chat. I always sat down to dinner with my boarders at 7:00.

Petunia jumped up on Jeremy's lap. He petted her behind the ears, and she began to purr gently, like a smoothly running engine. I watched his fingertips move softly over her fur. How was it that this mild young man had once parachuted in behind enemy lines and taken out Al-Qaida combatants? I wondered. I knew he had killed a lot of men. "Bad guys" is what they called them. "Yes, ma'am," he once told me, "when I was in the Army, I got rid of a hell of a lot of bad guys." How did these former soldiers turn off the killer instinct? How did they go from pulling triggers to caressing kittens? I had often pondered that question with respect to my boarders. Now, watching Jeremy, this good-natured young man, so attached to family, I had a hard time believing he had done what I knew he had done.

He was trying to put in as many hours as possible at the store, he told me, because he had to pay tuition. He would be starting night school in the fall, and the GI Bill wouldn't pay for everything. He certainly couldn't ask Mom and Dad for money. He was an adult, after all, nearly thirty-two years old. He had completed two years in a community college after he had come home from Iraq, but he still had two years left before he graduated. He'd have to take a reduced load because of work, but he planned to finish on time by taking courses in the summer. Then he would go to business school and get a real job. Dad had worked hard his whole life, Jeremy told me, and he had earned a rest. So no, he wouldn't be asking Dad for a dime.

"What about your mom?" I asked. "Does she work?" It seemed like an innocuous question.

"No," he said. "Dad never wanted her to work. She raised us four kids, and that was enough." His eyes had once again become inscrutable, stony. He had begun to pet Petunia more vigorously, and suddenly the cat gurgled and leapt off his lap. He watched her prowl through the grass and then disappear over the gate.

"Raising four children is no small thing," I said finally, and then added, "She's very beautiful."

"Oh yes, very beautiful. And lots of fun." He was staring at the rose, but I don't think he was really seeing it. "You know, I went into the Army right after high school," he murmured. "Dad didn't want me to. The war in Iraq was starting. He cried and cried. He was afraid."

"What about Mom?"

"She didn't say much, but I know she was scared too. To be honest, I gave them a lot of heartache. I never studied in high school. I cut classes. I fooled around. It never occurred to me to go to college back then. Dad wanted me to study. He wanted me to be an accountant because that's what he wanted to be, but he never got a chance to study. Now, I want to be an accountant too. Really, I do. But in those days, well, I guess I wasn't ready yet. Dad worked hard all day, physical labor. Now he's a manager, but in those days, he did heavy lifting. He'd come home with a sore back, sore legs, and I'd make fun of him. I was such an asshole. I feel like shit when I think back."

"You were just a kid."

"I put him through hell. Always in trouble. Always mouthing off to the teachers. Now, I want to have a career, but when I was eighteen, all I wanted was adventure, so I joined the Army. I was thrilled when they sent me to Iraq. Dad sobbed when I got my orders."

"I'm sure he's proud of you, Jeremy."

We sat there in silence awhile.

"Come on," I said finally. "Dinner is almost ready."

But Jeremy had entered his zone of melancholy. He sat staring at the blood-colored rose. I got up to go into the house.

In the fall, Jeremy stopped coming home for dinner. During the day, he worked at the hardware store. In the evening, he took classes in math and economics. During the weekend, he worked and studied.

"Take a break once in a while, Jeremy," I told him. "Come have dinner with us. After all, you have to eat."

"Right now, I have no time to eat. I'm like a crocodile. A croc can go three years without food, Mrs. M. Did you know that?"

"Bad idea, Jeremy."

"Don't worry about me, Mrs. M., I grab a sandwich here and there. Tell you what, Mrs. M. Someday I'll make you a *maja blanca*, a Philippine coconut pudding. Dad knows how to make it. I'll ask him to show me how when I visit him and Mom at Christmas."

"I wish I could meet your parents, Jeremy. They sound wonderful."

"Ah yes," he said. "Wonderful. I'm sure they'll come to my graduation. You can meet them then."

True to his word, Jeremy did graduate night school in two years. I wanted to have a graduation party for him, but he said that Mom and Dad had planned their own celebration.

"What about if I give a party at the house and they come too?" I suggested.

"Sorry, Mrs. M. They're going to take me to a fancy restaurant for dinner. But why don't you come to my graduation? You can meet them there."

Jeremy's graduation wasn't the first I'd attended. Over the years, several of my boarders had earned degrees. That day, I sat under the blazing sun and watched the hundreds of new graduates from the Continuing Education program parade down the aisles, then climb the stairs to the makeshift stage to receive their diplomas. When Jeremy's turn came, I cheered loudly, even though the dean had asked us to hold our applause until the end. I couldn't help it. I was so proud of him.

We had agreed to meet at the front gate of the university after the ceremony. As I approached, I recognized Jeremy's parents from a distance. Mom was just as lovely as in her photos. She wore a straw-colored suit of a shade that only a spectacular redhead could get away with. In the sunlight, her long copper-colored hair created a flaming aureole around her face.

"Mrs. Montez," said Jeremy, "I'd like you to meet my mother, Jenny."

Jenny turned to me without smiling and held out a limp hand.

"Jeremy says you've been very kind," she murmured. She had a voice like weak tea.

"And my father, Art."

Dad had cut off his ponytail and slicked back his hair. His strong arms bulged under his dark blue polyester jacket, obviously brand-new. He was beaming.

"Jeremy is the first one in the family to go to college," he told me. "And now he's going on to get his accounting degree at Cleveland

State. I thank God every day that he came home from the war sane and healthy. Well… healthy, except for the hip. But anyhow, now, he's a college graduate! And pretty soon, an accountant! He has told me so much about you, Mrs. Montez. Thank you for everything."

Jeremy went on to introduce his grandmother, his sister, his two brothers, and his aunt Magda. Then we said our good-byes. I watched them move down the street flanked by Mom and Dad. Art walked next to Jeremy, Jenny next to Magda. I was secretly disappointed that they hadn't invited me to accompany them to dinner or, at least, offered me a cup of coffee. After all, Jeremy had been living in my house for nearly two years. There were so many things I wanted to tell Jenny and Art about their wonderful son—how he got up at dawn to go to work, no matter how much his hip might be bothering him, how he studied until late at night, how sensitive and kind he was, and how much he loved them— he was always talking about Mom and Dad. Yes, especially that: how much he loved them. Although I was sure they already knew.

It was June again. Birds floated across the sky like petals wafted by a gentle breeze. Marigolds and zinnias competed for my attention and for their spot in the sun. The roses were more spectacular than ever. Two or three misses in frilly magenta ball gowns appeared every few days. Jeremy began packing up books and clothes to send off to Cleveland. He would keep his job at the hardware store until the end of the month, he told me, but then he would fly home to Ohio to find an apartment and get ready for business school.

I set the table for dinner and went out to get the mail. Few of my boarders received letters—they mostly used email—but that day, I fished a large white envelope with gold trim out of the mailbox. It had Jeremy's name on it.

I found him pulling books off the shelves and placing them carefully in boxes.

"There's a letter for you, Jeremy," I announced. "It looks like a wedding invitation. Maybe one of your Army buddies."

He caught his breath as I handed him the envelope. I turned to go, but he stopped me.

"Wait," he said. He had that familiar ashen look about him that always made me think his hip was bothering him. His fingers were trembling. He pulled out a card that looked like an announcement and read it slowly, probably several times, judging from the time it took him to react. He stared for a long time without moving, almost without breathing. Then, unexpectedly, his lips parted into a wide, sunny smile.

"It's Dad!" he said. "He's getting married!"

"What?"

He placed his hand on my shoulder with the same gentleness I had seen him cuddle Petunia.

"Let's have a glass of wine, Mrs. M. There's something I want to tell you."

We went into the kitchen and sat down. I noticed that his limp was more pronounced than usual that evening.

He waited for me to get settled and uncork the bottle.

"Mom and Dad are divorced," he said finally.

I blinked in disbelief.

"But... when? They were just here for your graduation."

"They separated while I was in Iraq—but they never told me. They knew it was a tough time for me. I was in one of the most violent spots in the country. They didn't want to upset or distract me. And then, I was injured."

"Jeremy, I can't believe it."

"I didn't know anything about it, so I

bought them a Hawaiian vacation, and... if you can believe it... they took it. They didn't want me to suspect anything. They emailed me dozens of photos from Honolulu. When I flew back home from Landstuhl, they were both at the airport, along with my brothers and sister. I didn't find out until that night. Dad came into my room and told me. I cried. I sobbed the way he had sobbed when I deployed."

Jeremy's voice broke. His cheeks were damp.

"I never mentioned it to you because..." He swallowed. "I just couldn't."

The tears were flowing now. The stoic warrior who had taken down scores of bad guys was, at that moment, as helpless as my kitten.

"They did it out of love, Mrs. M." He could hardly force out the words. "But now it's time for them both to move on."

He grimaced and crumpled his brow. He was in pain. All this time I had been worrying about his hip, but what really hurt him was something else: Mom and Dad.

The Last Mission

Only nine days left. Lt. Ignacio Montez would be leaving Iraq in a little more than a week, and he still had a lot left to do. There was Akram the carpenter, for example. The son of a bitch had hidden a bomb in a quiet intersection where kids liked to play soccer. It exploded and killed six innocent ten-year-olds. Then, there was Mahmod the sweeper. Barrel-shaped and soft-featured with the smile of a cherub, he looked like your favorite uncle, but he had gunned down a popular sheik in cold blood because the guy refused to cooperate with Al-Qaida. And what about Yazen the medic? The one who stuffed corpses with dynamite and then left them at the entrance to the souk or some other well-trafficked area. When a curious crowd—or better yet, a couple of American soldiers—gathered to examine the victim, Yazen would detonate the explosives. These were evil men, men who deliberately killed noncombatants. Montez had vowed that he and his Marines would catch them and bring them in, but so far, the thugs had eluded them. And then, there was Rahim the jeweler. Montez had to get to him, too. Montez glared at the calendar and bit his lip.

Akram was almost never in his carpenter's shop, but neighbors saw his wife, Noora, at the market, and she seemed to have money. No one was hiring Akram to build fences or ceiling moldings because no one was about to invest in property that might be blown up any moment. Besides, cash was tight. Lots of people were out of work. If Noora was parading around with fancy sandals and spending dinars on meat, Akram had to be getting cash from somewhere. Obviously, he was working for Al-Qaida, but the Marines didn't have much intel to go on. Even those people in this tight-knit little corner of Ramadi who hated Al-Qaida weren't willing to talk to the Americans. Al-Qaida was brutal, they thought, but the Americans were foreign occupiers.

Montez thought the deaths of the ten-year-olds might change things.

"I think folks are going to start talking, sir," Ken Pitney told Montez. "They've had it with the violence. They're not going to stand by while these motherfuckers murder their children."

Pitney was a thirty-seven-year-old staff

sergeant with twenty years in the military. A bulky black man with sharp perceptions and a fast draw, he had won six or eight medals for pulling Marines out of burning trucks or pushing them out of the line of fire. Montez felt ridiculous every time Pitney called him "sir," even though that was what military protocol required.

"I felt like I should be calling *him* 'sir,'" he once told me. "I was only twenty-four years old. He was the one with the experience, sometimes the only one who knew what the hell was going on."

Pitney was perpetually optimistic.

"The joy of the Lord courses through my veins," he told Montez, "especially when I'm about to go out on a raid."

"Well, we only have a week to catch Akram."

"His neighbors hate him. Someone's going to turn him in."

Montez thought Pitney might be right. Al-Qaida's diabolical tactic of killing children to coerce their parents' cooperation was becoming counterproductive. Sometimes the insurgents decapitated the kids and sometimes they shot them. Until now, parents had been so terrified they gave the thugs whatever they wanted—money, food, a place to hide men and supplies. But now, the buzz on the street was that a rebellion was brewing.

Akram's job was to plant bombs in places where youngsters gathered: streets where they played soccer or marbles, storefronts with television sets. Neighbors whispered that his mission gave him some kind of personal catharsis: he took out his anger against Allah for giving him only daughters by killing other people's sons.

As usual, Pitney was right.

"He's going to go home tonight," he told Montez. "That's what they say."

"Who says?"

"Bab the clothier. The one who sells kaftans. You know, the one with pustules."

"The guy with a face like a potato with eyes sprouting out all over it?"

"Yeah. Bab overheard Akram's cousin say something. Bab lost a nephew to one of Akram's bombs. That's why he told me. Like I said, sir, people are fed up."

At 3:00 a.m., Montez and his team were creeping through the shadows to the modest house attached to Akram's shop. A gloomy moon offered feeble light, but darkness was a blessing. If the Marines were lucky, they'd catch the carpenter in his sleep. Pitney would be in the most danger because he was in the lead position. Akram was surely armed, and if he was awake, he'd fire at the first moving silhouette he saw. He probably had armed guards. If so, they'd pull the women and children in front of them to prevent the Marines from firing. It was also possible that Noora would have a pistol as well.

Revolver drawn, Montez kicked in the door as noiselessly as possible.

"The first split second is always the worst," Ignacio told me. "You never know what to expect. It might be a barrage of fire. It might be a lone gunman."

Ignacio held his breath. Pitney was already inside. One by one, four other Marines followed. They met no resistance. That could mean Akram and his guys were waiting for all of them to enter the house to mow them down, or it could mean the house was booby-trapped and would blow up any minute.

Pitney turned on a low-beam flashlight. Four little girls appeared to be deep in slumber on the floor, each on a mat.

"They looked like angels," said Ignacio, "their hair spilling over their shoulders, their tiny noses spreading and contracting, their delicately arched eyebrows, their ears like perfectly tied bows. Please, God, I thought, don't let anything happen to these children."

Pitney looked around the room. No Akram. No Noora.

He signaled two Marines to follow him and went to check out the rest of the house. Ignacio and two others stayed by the entrance guarding the girls. Pitney examined the walls for false doors leading to rooms where a person or weapons could be hidden. He checked the perimeter. Nothing.

Ignacio closed the door carefully, and they left.

"Well, that was anticlimactic," he muttered.

"But isn't that the damnedest thing?" murmured Pitney. "We searched the whole house and those little girls never woke up."

"Too bad Akram wasn't there."

"We have eight more days."

"We have intel that Mahmod the sweeper is hiding in the mosque."

"Crap," growled Pitney. "I hate to go into the mosque."

"Yeah, me too. It's their sacred space, but we're going to have to. I just hope we can find Akram and Yazen within the next couple of days. And then there's Rahim the jeweler."

"Rahim isn't so important."

"Yeah, he is. It's a personal thing."

The moon was dying. They had to check

out the mosque and get back to base by daybreak. Montez imagined he would be busy all day getting their quarters ready to turn over to the next battalion, and of course, they had to train the new men.

"None of us have slept for thirty-six hours, sir. With all due respect, I think you should forget about Rahim."

"You guys can sleep a couple of hours when we get back, Pitney. I'll visit Rahim."

The mosque operation turned out to be easy. They found Mahmod the sweeper prostrate in prayer, alone and in full view.

"He just shot an innocent man, a sheik that the whole fucking neighborhood loved," hissed Pitney. "For sure, God is going to tell him to piss off."

"Who knows what God is going to do? Surround him, but let him finish."

The minute he lifted his head, Mahmod knew it was all over. He didn't even reach for his gun. Ignacio handcuffed him and threw him into the truck. He followed Ignacio into the interrogation room like a lamb waiting for the knife.

"Not so bad," Montez told Captain Parodi, the commanding officer. "One out of three. And then, of course, there's Rahim."

"Forget Rahim. There's no time."

"I'll make time for Rahim," said Montez, tightening his jaw. He began to write up his report on Mahmod.

At 3:00 a.m. the next morning, Montez's team was on its way to an abandoned shack on the outskirts of Ramadi. That was where Yazen the medic brought the corpses to perform his gruesome operation. He slit the bodies from breastbone to pubis, removed the guts, and filled the cavity with explosives to be detonated at the moment when they could produce the most horror. He had a bunch of assistants, seasoned killers known to be crack shots. Montez brought a bigger team with him than the night before.

"They're heavily armed. Guns, RPGs, you name it," Pitney told Montez. "We might need air cover."

Yazen's men had either been tipped off or seen them coming. They fired the first shot.

Ignacio didn't tell me the details. He never talks about the gore of battle. All I know is that the firefight lasted more than four hours. Yazen had more men with him than Ignacio had anticipated. I can imagine the screaming bullets, the flying debris. In my mind, I can smell the sweat and the burning flesh. In the end, Yazen lay dead over one of his cadavers. Most of his men met the same fate. A few were captured. One of the Marines caught a bullet in the shoulder and another had his hand blown to dust. By the time Ignacio attended to the injured and handed over the detainees, he'd slept less than five hours in two-and-a-half days. The computer, the printer, and the paperweight on his desk all seemed to dissolve into each other. It was like watching ice sculptures melt in a desert, he said. He put his head on his desk and slept.

It was only a catnap, but that's all he had time for. Twenty minutes later, he was off to patrol the souk with Shem the interpreter and three Marines.

"We're going in here," he said, when they reached the shop of Rahim the jeweler.

Rahim, by all accounts, was a gentle man, good-natured and big-hearted, but no friend to Americans. He stared warily at the four heavily armed infantrymen entering his shop.

"Wait outside," said Montez to the Marines. "I'll stay here with Shem."

"*As-salām 'alaykum,*" said Montez to the jeweler.

Rahim's eyes grew large and seemed to spin like pinwheels.

"Tell him I'd like to buy a necklace," Montez said to Shem.

He removed his helmet so the jeweler

could see his face. Then he put down his guns, his knife, his rucksack, and even his flak jacket. Now he was just a man, not a solider.

"I'm leaving in a few days," he explained, "and I want to buy a present for my mother."

Without taking his eyes off Montez, Rahim took out five gold necklaces and laid them a black velvet cloth. Exquisite pieces. Delicate gold filigree, laden with intricate twirls and arabesques.

Montez made his selection. He knew he was supposed to haggle, but he didn't have much time.

"I wish you peace and happiness," Montez said after they had decided on a price and he was getting ready to leave. Rahim's features softened. He could certainly understand a young man's affection for his mother.

"I wish you the same," he said.

Ignacio gave me the necklace for my birthday, when he told me this story. It was hard for me to hold back the tears—to think that in the middle of a war, he had remembered to buy his mother a birthday gift.

"Did you get Akram?" I asked finally.

"Unfortunately not," he said. "But at least I got to Rahim."

Ahmed the Tailor

Ahmed hated Americans. He'd lost his young nephew and two cousins during the early months of the invasion, and he held the Americans responsible for the violence and chaos that ravaged his country. He knew that Al-Qaida operatives, not Americans, had planted the bomb that had blown up Yasin, a gangling sixteen-year-old with dreams of becoming a politician. Zamir, on the other hand, had fallen victim to an American sniper, and Hasan had died when a car exploded at a checkpoint in Ramadi. None of this would have happened if the Americans hadn't invaded Iraq, thought Ahmed, and now, to make matters worse, some of his Sunni brothers had switched sides. They had joined the Sunni Awakening, supporting the Marines in their drive against Al-Qaida. According to these turncoats, Al-Qaida did even more harm than the Americans. It was Al-Qaida who terrorized the populace, they said, decapitating children to intimidate their parents, blowing up schools and marketplaces to keep people cowering in their homes. Of course, they said, no one wanted foreigners overrunning the land, but if you had to choose between the Americans and Al-Qaida, the Americans were the lesser of two evils.

Ahmed wasn't buying any of it. It was the Americans' fault, he kept saying. It was all the Americans' fault. No one was coming into his tailor's shop, and it was because in the middle of a war, the last thing people thought about was buying a new suit. And who had caused this stupid war, anyway? The Americans!

"Things will change," his wife, Kayoosh, told him. "Ramadi is more peaceful now. Soon people will buy." At least, that's what I imagine she said.

It was true that the streets were quieter. Now that the Awakening was taking hold and the U.S. government had sent more soldiers—the "surge," they called it—you could walk through the souk without fear that a bomb might explode under your feet. Some of the neighbors even liked the Americans. The men in uniform handed out candy and soccer balls to the children, and a few of them had learned some Arabic.

"They're killers!" snarled Ahmed.

"In wartime, everybody's a killer," said Kayoosh calmly.

"Well, I hate them! Candy and soccer balls

don't make up for the deaths of three blood relatives!"

"You may have to take up sewing *disdashas*."

"I'm not sewing *disdashas*," snapped Ahmed, referring to the long, kaftan-like garments worn by many Iraqi men and most women. "My father made top-quality, British-style suits, and his father before him. That's what I know how to do."

Ahmed sat in his shop and waited. He didn't go to the brotherhood meetings, where men talked about the Awakening and how best to keep Al-Qaida away. He didn't associate with neighbors who informed Marines about who was harboring insurgents or stockpiling weapons. He just sat in his shop, surrounded by bolts of superb English wool, and waited.

No one came.

I didn't know Ahmed, of course. My son Ignacio told me about him on one of those rare occasions when he talked about his time in Iraq. He never told war stories—the kind they show on television, where Americans kick in doors and get the bad guys. I imagine Ignacio kicked in doors too, during his first deployment, but by his second tour, many Sunnis were cooperating with the Marines, and the Americans reciprocated by rebuilding the town. They constructed schools and souks, set up medical centers, repaved the streets, and painted the water tower. That gave Ignacio the chance to meet people and make friends—but not with Ahmed. Ahmed wouldn't talk to the Marines. He wouldn't allow his boys to play with the American soccer balls they handed out. When he saw the neighborhood children crowding around soldiers and trying out their English—"Hello, my name is Sham!" "Hello, I like candy!"—he walked by in a hurry. When he saw the Americans clowning around—for example, plopping their helmets down on the heads of seven-year-olds, who squealed with glee—he looked away.

Ignacio had heard about Ahmed. He met periodically with the sheiks to discuss security concerns and building projects, and occasionally, Ahmed's name came up. Ahmed the tailor, who hated Americans. Ahmed, who probably didn't have any information about Al-Qaida, but you could never tell. You had to be careful. People who held grudges could be dangerous.

Ignacio knew where Ahmed's shop was. It was in the souk, attached to his house, between the rug seller and the stall that sold cheap T-shirts.

"I think I'll pay him a visit," said Ignacio.

"Don't bother," said one of the elders. "He won't talk to you. He won't even let you in."

In my mind, I conjure up an image of Ahmed. I see a man of about forty, aged by war and worry. His face, an elongated oval. His skin, rutted copper. Short, black hair. Heavy eyebrows. Moustache. Cleft chin. Lackluster forehead. Intelligent eyes that draw me in, the eyes of a seer lost in a revelation. A solid but disordered body, like that of a broken boxer.

I imagine Ignacio sauntering up to that unwelcoming house. He can see Ahmed, the gloomy tailor, through the shattered window. He can see the bolts of fabric, the outmoded sewing machine, the bobbins, the thimbles. He can see Ahmed's boys, aged eight and ten, playing with empty spools. Ignacio knocks.

Ahmed hesitates, then gets up to open the door. He might as well open it, he probably thinks, because Ignacio can kick it in if he wants to. Actually, Ignacio won't kick it in because that's all over now. The Awakening has mostly put an end to kicking in doors. Even so, in Ahmed's mind, you can never know about Americans, so he opens it.

"Good morning," says Ignacio in Arabic.

"I'm Lieutenant Ignacio Montez."

Ahmed squints at him through twisted spectacles.

"I'd like to have a suit made."

"A suit?" I asked my son. "Did you need a suit? In Ramadi?"

"I needed him to let me in," said Ignacio. "I thought this was the most effective way."

Ahmed stares at Ignacio a long time. Ignacio assumes he is sizing up the situation, deciding whether to trust him. But no, Ahmed is taking mental measurements, calculating yardage. He is clearly seething, but a job is a job. He hasn't had an order in months.

"Stand over here," he barks, pointing to a small platform in front of a filmy full-length mirror.

"It needs to be resilvered," says Ignacio in English, but Ahmed doesn't understand, and Ignacio doesn't know how to say it in Arabic.

Ignacio is wearing no weapons but a sidearm, but two Marines are standing guard outside the shop in case of trouble. Once Ahmed begins maneuvering the measuring tape across his back, down his arm, down his leg, Ignacio is sure that there will be no trouble. The man is clearly a master, a perfectionist—slow, methodical, precise. He assesses Ignacio's shape and stance. He measures each leg separately.

"Sit down," says Ahmed. "You will choose fabric."

In addition to the bolts of fine English wool, there are books with sample swatches. Ahmed wants to know where the suit will be worn, whether it must be suitable for a temperate climate or snow or the desert, whether it will be for summer or winter. Does Ignacio want pure wool? Gabardine or merino? Herringbone or sharkskin? A silk blend? Lightweight wool is good for the warm weather, he explains. And what about the color? What about the price?

Ahmed wants the equivalent of three hundred dollars for the grey gabardine suit that Ignacio picks out. Ignacio knows that a made-to-order garment of fine wool could cost a thousand dollars back home, but he also knows that he has to bargain. Ahmed expects it. He won't respect the American if he doesn't put up a fight. A dollar is worth a little less than 2,000 dinars. Neither man wants to calculate the price in tens of thousands of dinars, so they agree to negotiate in U.S. currency.

"One hundred," offers Ignacio.

"That's ridiculous! I have a family to feed!" counters Ahmed.

"One hundred ten."

"You're insulting me! Two hundred ninety!"

The negotiations go on for over an hour, during which Ahmed orders his ten-year-old to bring tea. Finally, they agree on two hundred dollars.

"Come back in three days," says Ahmed.

"When I tried it on and looked in the mirror, I felt like some kind of a fashion model from the eighties," Ignacio told me. "The suit was gorgeous, exquisitely styled although a bit outmoded. After all, Ramadi isn't the style capital of the Middle East, and Ahmed didn't have access to the latest patterns. But crap, Mom, it fit perfectly!" He carried it back to base and hung it on a hanger on a hook on the wall.

Nothing changed. Ahmed continued to stay away from neighborhood meetings and he continued to badmouth Americans. When the neighborhood kids crowded around the Marines for candy and soccer balls, Ahmed's sons weren't among them.

A few weeks later, Ignacio trudged back down the road to the souk past rows of bullet-pocked houses. He noticed that some people had begun repairing walls and painting doors. There was no sense in making repairs when bombs were going off up and down the street, but now that things were calmer, roses (yes, roses!) in pots had appeared in front of some of the houses, and rays of sunlight were settling on windows framed with swirly organdy curtains.

Ahmed opened the door right away this time. "I need another suit," explained Ignacio. "When I get back home, I'll be wearing suits every day."

"Ah," said Ahmed. He took the tape measure from his teeth and put it down. "I already have the measurements."

"It needs to be resilvered," said Ignacio, pointing to the mirror. Actually, he said, "It needs to be repaired with silver on the back." He had learned the word in Arabic for "silver" and had practiced the sentence for several hours.

"Yes," said Ahmed, "but that's expensive."

Three days later Ahmed produced another beautiful suit, this one a blue merino number. Ignacio put it on and modeled it for the other lieutenants.

"Classy, Montez," said Ray Crenshaw, Ignacio's friend since training at Twenty-Nine Palms.

"A little old-fashioned, don't you think? I

mean, with those pleats in the front."

"I don't know nothing about fashion and neither does anyone else in Moosebridge, South Dakota, where I come from. But I sure wouldn't mind having a suit like that for weddings and stuff."

Ignacio hung the blue suit on the hook with the gray one and waited.

"You're wasting your time," said Crenshaw. "The guy'll take your money, but he still hates Americans."

The sheiks said the same thing. Ignacio went to community meetings to discuss ways in which the local people and the Marines could work together, but Ahmed never showed up. The sheiks who visited the tailor couldn't get him to change his mind. Who knew if he wasn't in cahoots with Al-Qaida? they said.

Before long, Ignacio was once again trudging up the street to Ahmed's shop, this time with Crenshaw.

"*As-salam alaykom*," said Ignacio, when Ahmed opened the door. "I need a lightweight suit for when I get back. My friend, Lieutenant Crenshaw, wants one, too."

For the first time, Ahmed smiled. "Please sit down and look through the pattern books," he said to Ignacio cordially.

"That's quite a lot of money for suits," I said to my son.

"I thought it was a good investment, Mom."

"Well, you need suits for job interviews, now that you're out of the military."

"I needed Ahmed to cooperate with us."

The tailor took Crenshaw's measurements.

"Where are your boys?" asked Ignacio. "They're usually here with you."

"They went back to school. They've reopened the secular madrassas. All the children are in school, even the girls."

Ignacio was glad to hear it. He'd helped rebuild those schools destroyed by war.

"Tea?" asked Ahmed, when he was done taking the order.

Instead of calling for Kayoosh, he led the men into the main part of the house, where cushions were arranged on a carpet. Ignacio and Crenshaw sat on the floor cross-legged. Before long, Kayoosh floated in like a specter, barefaced but eyes lowered. A plain white *dishdasha* covered her from neck to toe. On her head, she wore a black hijab.

"She was a beauty," remarked Ignacio. "High, sculpted cheekbones, skin the shade of light brown sugar."

Ahmed's traumatized old house was smashed and splintered on the outside, but inside hung tapestries of red, gold, green, and white, some a riot of flowers crowded against solid backgrounds, some an interweaving of arabesques and curlicues.

I imagine Kayoosh gliding across the room. I see her standing against the ornate walls, an elegant black-and-white onyx in a box of gaudy baubles. I imagine Ignacio straining to sip his tea and divert his gaze away from her face.

What can a mother do but imagine? When Ignacio went to Iraq for the second time, I knew little about the Awakening. I imagined him dodging bullets and bombs, as he had during his earlier deployment. I think that all mothers whose children are far away in exotic and dangerous places spend their lives imagining the worst. Now I imagine a different scene: Kayoosh cocooned in white, her smooth face framed in indigo. Kayoosh crouching by the Americans with a carved wooden tray upon which she has placed a teapot, three cups, and a plate of sweets. Ignacio knows that Ahmed has been out of work for a long time. Sweets are a luxury, a sacrifice he has made for his guests.

Ignacio comments on the loveliness of the

wall hangings. They have been in the family for generations, explains Ahmed. Ignacio is careful not to comment on the loveliness of the hostess or even to acknowledge her presence.

"Do you think," says Ahmed after a while, "that other Americans might want suits?"

"Maybe," says Ignacio. He must be careful not to give the impression he is bargaining: more work for cooperation with the Marines.

"Perhaps you have other friends who…"

"I will ask," says Ignacio quietly.

Within a week or so, a trickle of Marines, mostly enlisted men, began to make their way to Ahmed's tailor shop.

I imagine Kayoosh saying to her husband, "You know, in war bad things happen to everyone. It's not usually the fault of the men sent to do the fighting. Why don't you try working with the Americans? As soldiers go, they're not particularly cruel, and after all, they're bringing you business."

I don't know whether she actually said those things or not, but Ignacio told me that after that, every time he passed the tailor shop, he saw Ahmed busy at his sewing machine. Occasionally, the tailor would look up and see Ignacio through the window. He would smile and wave, and often he would invite him in for tea.

About six weeks before he redeployed to the States, Ignacio began scouting around for a mirror.

"Where the hell are you going to find a thing like that?" laughed Crenshaw.

"I'll ask around the souk. Someone will know."

The carpenter Mustafa suggested they try his cousin Ali's antiques shop. The front of the shop had been badly damaged by a grenade, but miraculously Ali had salvaged a few treasures he kept in a storage area in the back—among them, a large, oval mirror with a wooden frame decorated with interlocking triangles. It was fastened to a stand with hinges on either side that permitted the mirror to tilt. Two smaller side mirrors, each in the shape of a half oval, folded inward over the main glass, creating a large decorative panel. Ignacio haggled with Ali an hour or so. Then he and Crenshaw carried the purchase to Ahmed's shop.

Ahmed looked at the mirror as though it were an apparition. His eyes had the pained look of a martyr at the rack.

"Come," he said finally. "I'll ask Kayoosh to bring tea."

The three men sat on the floor and sipped.

"It won't make me work with the Americans," said Ahmed after a while.

"It's a gift," said Ignacio softly. "I expect nothing in return."

"A nephew and two cousins," said Ahmed with a sigh. "The boy had a future. He would have gone to school, maybe become a lawyer, maybe a politician. And my cousins were like brothers to me."

"I understand."

"You can't understand."

"I want you to have the mirror, Ahmed. I've spent many enjoyable hours here with you. I wanted to give you a present, that's all."

"Thank you," Ahmed said softly. "It's a beautiful mirror, and very useful for my work."

Ignacio and Ray got up to leave. Ahmed embraced Ignacio, kissing him on both cheeks. "You're a good man," whispered Ahmed. "You helped me get my business going again. But war causes bad blood."

Ignacio squeezed Ahmed's hand. "Peace can make good blood," he whispered.

Then Ahmed embraced Crenshaw, and the Americans left.

* * *

The new unit of Marines was settling in,

and Ignacio and his men were packing up. Days remained before they were to climb into trucks for the first leg of the journey home. From Baghdad, they would fly to Dublin and from there, to Charlotte, South Carolina.

Ignacio was addressing mailing labels when Crenshaw came running in.

"Hey, Ig! You'll never guess what I just saw!"

"An Iraqi woman in a bikini," muttered Ignacio dryly.

"I saw Ahmed walking toward the big Marine base, Hurricane Point! And you know what he was carrying? Swatches of fabric! Pattern books! His tailor's kit with measuring tapes and pins and stuff! He's going to sell his wares to the Marines!"

Ignacio chuckled. "He's a good person, Ray. You can't blame him for being bitter, but all Ahmed really wants is to work. Working is the only thing that will help him get through his grief. Anyhow, I hope he sees now that we gringos aren't such bad guys. And maybe eventually… eventually…"

I imagine Ahmed trudging up the dusty street, impeccably dressed in herringbone tweed despite the 108-degree morning sun. The tight weave of creases around his eyes slightly relaxed. His lips parted in an anticipatory smile. I see him explaining his business to the sentries, showing the gate pass secured for him by Lt. Ignacio Montez, shifting his sample swatches from one arm to another to show his ID, passing inside.

I imagine him back home, sipping tea in a room filled with ornate tapestries, orange, gold, green, and red, tightly packed with geometric designs and graceful Arabic writing. I imagine him embracing Ignacio, kissing his cheeks and murmuring, "You helped me get my business going again. *Assalamu Alaikom warahmatu Allahi wa barakatuhu.*"

"May God bless you as well."

* * *

It was a few months after Ignacio left the Marines that a package came, a rectangular box with a New Hampshire address. I called Ignacio at work.

"Who is it from?" he asked.

"The name in the corner is Rick Sabatini."

"Hmm, I don't know anyone by that name." I heard a barely perceptible tremor in his voice.

I began to worry. After Ignacio had returned from his first tour in Iraq, a package came with the shoes of a Marine killed in action. A young man named Ryan McCall who had been a good friend of Ignacio's. Ryan had said that if anything happened to him, he wanted my son to have his shoes. I didn't really understand, and Ignacio never explained, but he kept the shoes in his closet, always dusted and perfectly shined.

When Ignacio got home, he looked at the package for what seemed like an eternity, turning it over and staring at the address. Then he tore it open.

It was a suit. Perfectly tailored wool gabardine. The note read in Arabic: "For Lt. Ignacio Montez. From your friend, Ahmed."

Ahmed had given it to one of the men in the unit that replaced Ignacio's and asked him to send it to my son.

* * *

Now I look at the television screen, at the images of ISIS fighters garbed in black, knives in hand, and I remember that once there were two men from radically different worlds who sat on cushions and drank tea together. And I wonder where Ahmed is now.

Upside Down

The day my son told me he was deploying to Iraq, my world turned upside down. The dust cloth fell from my hand. The clock stopped ticking, specks of dirt hovered midair, and the sparrow on the sill morphed into a plaster statuette. I remember that the room started to spin, and the ceiling fixtures were suddenly where the carpet should have been. I felt nauseous. I put my hand to my mouth.

"When?"

"Come on, Mom," said Ignacio. "You knew I was going to have to go. Don't be a drama queen."

Is that what he thought? I wondered. That I was being a drama queen? Do these smart-ass kids have any idea of the terror a mother feels when her child goes to war?

"When?" I asked again.

"August."

"It'll be hot," I said stupidly.

"Especially with a flak jacket and 100 pounds of gear on my back."

"Oh God," I whispered.

"You don't notice when the bullets are fly..." He stopped. "You don't notice when you're busy." He laughed as though he'd said something amusing.

I put down the cloth and turned to him, but he was already out of the room. We were not going to talk about it. That was clear.

* * *

I thought about Iraq incessantly. At the bank, as I handed the customers their cash. At the market, as I examined the cantaloupe. In the shower, as I watched the drops trickle down my increasingly flaccid thighs.

I poured over library books. "Iraq is the cradle of civilization," I read. "It was once called Mesopotamia, the land between the rivers—the Euphrates and the Tigris." The photographs mesmerized me. The Euphrates, a dazzling, undulating, blue ribbon of water against an orange sky so radiant that it made your eyes burn. (Even the picture made your eyes burn.) Row upon row of palm trees crowned by a fiery sphere of gold with a center of molten pearl. Stretches of green, lush and rich. Poplars, willows, camel thorn. Reeds and rushes. The Garden of Eden, after all. "A young boy herds sheep in Nasiriya," I read. Above was a photo of a kaftan-clad child of eleven or twelve, surrounded by a throng of sheep. I turned the pages. Sheep and goats. Gazelle and river otters. Cheetahs and wild donkeys.

The chapter called "Culture" showed a pastry shop in Mosul with trays of sugary sweets. Children in festive outfits of red and green at a party during Eid al-Fitr. I wondered: What is it really like over there? What has war done to this country? Ignacio had sent me photos, too. Boys carrying platters of biscuits on their heads. Souks with rows of brightly colored vegetables—ruby red pomegranates, oranges swollen with nectar, grapes like piles of jade marbles. Most of his photos were of children. Little girls, with their shy smiles, peeking out from gracefully arched doors. Little boys playing soccer. No bleeding corpses. No wailing mothers. Ignacio had censured the images just as the editors of the books had.

But the newspapers and websites told a different story. They showed shattered buildings and shattered skulls, snipers taking aim, men being blown from turrets, guards holding down prisoners, hospitals teeming with broken bodies, blood seeping into the sand, soldiers weeping over the wrecked torsos of children, coffins. Lots of coffins.

My doctor, Mary, prescribed a broadcast blackout.

"No newspapers," she said. "No TV. You're driving yourself crazy, Jacqueline."

"No, I'm fine."

"Maybe something to calm you down…"

"I don't need it."

"Do you sleep?"

"Never. I just lie in bed and listen to the explosions in my head."

"Valium, maybe. Just until you can get back into a normal sleeping routine. You need to rest, Jacqueline."

"What good will it do for me to be calm if people are killing each other over there? Will my calm protect my son in a firefight?"

"Your being a wreck won't protect him, either."

"I don't want to be calm because I'm drugged. I want to be calm because the war is over, and everybody is safe."

She considered my logic.

"Okay," she said. "At least try some warm milk before bed and keep doing yoga. Exercise is good for you. And stay away from the newscasts."

I requested daily alerts from the *New York Times*. Keywords: Ramadi. Iraq. Marines.

My yoga teacher, Anne, prescribed

meditation. "Relax," she said. "Breathe deeply."

Instead, I joined Adopt-a-Platoon and became a platoon mother.

"How many do you want?" asked the woman on the phone.

"Three."

"Three soldiers?"

"Three platoons."

"That's probably going to be about 60 or 70 soldiers, dear. That's far too many."

I insisted, and she gave them to me. Two Army platoons (Iraq and Afghanistan) and one of Marines (Iraq). In addition to Ignacio's.

I wrote letters constantly, three or four a day. If the platoon had internet access, I wrote emails. I baked like a demon and bought boatloads of socks that I packed, along with the cookies, into Priority-Mail boxes. I bought soap, shampoo, baby wipes, Purell, granola bars, coffee, and football magazines. The sergeants wrote back to me. They sent me photos of their soldiers and sometimes of their families. They told me which cookies they liked the best. They were courteous and appreciative, but I knew I was doing it as much for myself as for them.

Sometimes I'd see a woman at the post office with boxes labeled APO or FPO—

military addresses. I'd approach and ask her about her soldier—sometimes a son or daughter, a father, a husband, or a sibling. Once one of the women burst into tears. I hugged her and let her cry on my shoulder.

Jennifer, the postal clerk, had two sons in Afghanistan. Sometimes she gave me tips about what to send. The Purell was her idea.

"Sometimes they don't have access to water," she said. "With Purell, they can at least clean their hands."

"Wow!" she exclaimed one morning when I showed up with five stuffed boxes. "You're keeping the Post Office alive!"

"Actually," I said, "the Post Office is keeping *me* alive."

A while later, when she was going over the customs form, she noticed that I'd included several bags of kibble and dog treats. Ignacio and his men had adopted a dog and named him Ox.

"What's this?" she said, scowling.

"Purina and Milk Bones."

"You can't send Purina and Milk Bones. They're not allowed to keep pets over there."

"I know," I said. "But they've taken in this stray..."

Without flinching, she picked up her marker, blacked out "dog treats," and wrote in "cookies."

Every week I'd stare at the young faces in "Faces of the Fallen" in the newspaper, terrified I'd see someone I knew. Every day I'd check the casualty statistics and calculate Ignacio's chances of survival. I'd think: there are 187,000 troops over there. Last week, 49 died. Way less than one percent. That meant he had better than a 99 percent chance of making it through in one piece. For a moment, I'd feel better, but then, I'd think, what difference do the odds make if it's your kid who gets hit?

I never tried to justify the war. I couldn't think about the politics of it. All I wanted was for my son to come home healthy and whole.

Occasionally Ignacio called.

"One of my guys wants to apply to college," he told me over the satellite phone. "Could you send some SAT prep books, Mom?"

"Sure," I said. "How are you? What are you doing?"

"Everything's fine. Just another day at work."

There was no point in insisting.

Suddenly there was a *bam*. I was sure it was an explosion.

"What was that!?" I shouted into the

phone. "It sounded like a grenade or something!"

"No, no. Someone just slammed the door." He was laughing. I was trembling.

He called again right after Thanksgiving.

"I saw on the television that they had a nice dinner for the troops," I said. "Did you have turkey and cranberry sauce?"

"That's only on TV, Mom. I was out, but don't worry about it. I had enough to eat."

I was out. I knew that meant he was off on a raid and that I shouldn't ask questions.

Every time I read about a calamity, I'd email him. "I read there was an attack on a government building. Are you OK, Ignacio? Please answer!" "I read that a bunch of IEDs went off along a main thoroughfare they call Michigan Avenue. Are you OK? Please answer!" "I heard there were casualties at a checkpoint in the western sector. Is that near you? Are you OK? PLEASE ANSWER!

"Please, Mom," he wrote back. "Whatever you read in the papers is a bunch of crap. If anything happens to me, they'll notify you."

I turned off the computer and cried.

He didn't tell me when his friend Fitz was blown up by an IED. I read it in "Faces of the Fallen."

"He didn't make it," was all Ignacio said

when I asked about it. His voice was even, as though he were talking about someone who had set off for a football game and never got there because he ran into a traffic jam. "He didn't make it."

I prayed a lot, and I did a lot of yoga. In fact, I did yoga every single day. Not the meditations that Anne, the instructor, had suggested, but hardcore *asanas*—that's what they call yoga poses. I did all the *asanas* except one: the handstand. I just couldn't flip myself upside down.

My downward facing dogs were passable, and my flank stretch was pretty good. My Warrior 1 was nicely aligned, and I could get into tree pose, even though I couldn't hold it very long. I could even do a headstand. However, every time Anne announced, "*Adho Mukha Vrksasana*," I shuddered.

"Don't worry about it," said Anne. "You've got a lot on your mind."

"What do you want to do a handstand for at your age?" chided Mary. "Stretching is good for you, but standing on your hands? Don't make yourself crazy about this, Jacqueline! You're already under too much stress. What's the point of setting impossible goals for yourself?"

As usual, I didn't listen to her. If Ignacio

could fight Al-Qaida in Iraq, I thought, the very least I could do was learn to do a handstand. "He's risking his life to fight bad guys," I told myself. "I should be able to accomplish this one little thing. I'm going to learn to do a handstand in his honor!"

I expected Anne to be indifferent or even hostile. After all, I thought, she's a yoga instructor —one of those hippie-dippie pacifists who think that military mothers are all warmongers and don't realize that *we* are not the ones who chose to go to war. But she surprised me.

"That's a great idea," she said. "It'll give you something to concentrate on until Ignacio gets home."

I tensed. "If he gets home," I whispered. But then I pushed that thought out of my mind.

Every week in class, Anne asked us all to place our hands against the wall with our rumps up and our feet as close to our hands as possible.

"An inverted V," she said.

I bent my body into an inverted V.

"Now kick up," she said.

I bent my knees and with all my strength thrust my feet upward. My right foot lifted about eighteen inches off the ground and the left foot just a smidgeon. Then both feet jerked back down to the yoga mat.

"Next time!" said Anne cheerily.

"I can't do it!"

"You can't do it *today!* Next time you'll do it."

Yoga-speak for "klutz," I thought.

Every week in class, I tried. At home, I tried several times a day. Before work. Before dinner. Before bed. I'd close the door, position myself by the wall, and kick up. Nothing.

"You're getting there," Anne kept saying. "Your kicks are getting better."

"Well, I'm not doing a handstand," I said sourly.

"Look," she said finally, "try to kick up and I'll catch your legs and put you into an inverted position just so you can see how it feels. That way, you'll have a better idea of what you're aiming for."

Dutifully, I knelt and kicked. She caught my ankles and held them by the wall. I looked out at the upside-down world and felt a sudden rush of exhilaration. But the instant she let go, I fell.

"You did it!" she said.

"No, I didn't. You were holding me."

"Barely. You're getting stronger, Jacqueline. Soon you'll do it."

One day, while I was practicing at home, Ignacio called.

"You'll never guess what I'm doing," I told him. "I'm learning to do a handstand."

"Okay, Mom," he said after a brief silence, "if that's what you want."

"In your honor. I'll be able to do it by the time you come home!"

More silence.

"You'll be so proud when you see what a kick-ass yogi I've become!"

"Sure, Mom."

Then he thanked me for the cookies I'd sent and told me how much the men had enjoyed them. I decided not to let his lack of enthusiasm sidetrack me.

A couple of days later, I noticed an announcement for a handstand workshop with the arm-balance specialist at the yoga studio. I signed up.

"Wonderful idea!" said Anne.

"Don't overdo," said Mary. "I don't want you to have a heart attack!"

The specialist had us stand in a doorway in an inverted V, back against one jamb, and then walk up the opposite jamb until we were almost vertical. I did it but couldn't go from there to a full arm balance. Then she had us stand in an inverted V with our backs almost against the wall and kick up from there. She showed us different ways to kick up—straight knee, bent knee—and different ways to position our wrists.

"How was the workshop?" asked Anne during our next class.

"I still can't do it."

"It'll come," she said.

Liar! I thought.

Every morning I counted the days until Ignacio's probable return. They never give you an exact date, but I was using his birthday, March 30, as a goal for my handstand. Surely, he'll be home by then, I thought. A million newspaper articles collided in my mind, the ones about soldiers who stepped on IEDs a day before they were supposed to redeploy, the ones about helicopter accidents on the way to the airfield where soldiers were supposed to catch their flight home. I pushed them out of my mind, headed back to the wall, and took an inverted V position.

Ignacio telephoned again not long before he was supposed to leave Iraq.

"I can't tell you when, but it won't be long," he said.

"Listen," I said. "I'm still trying, but so far I haven't been able to do a handstand."

He chuckled. "Don't worry about it, Mom. And please, don't hurt yourself."

I was disappointed that I hadn't realized my goal, but all that mattered was that he was coming home.

"Damn the handstand!" I said aloud. "Dear God, please keep him safe!"

On March 26, I was in the kitchen cleaning up, when the phone rang. Warm water ran over glistening ceramic. Fragrant foam accumulated on the walls of the basin. It occurred to me that soon crocuses would be blooming. It was a bright, late winter day. Rays streamed through the windows, washing the walls in liquid sunlight. Everything seemed so normal, and yet, I was afraid to think that it was, afraid to relax and enjoy the heralds of spring.

The phone rang again. I put down the sponge and turned off the water. It rang a third time. I held my breath.

"Hello, Mom?"

"Ig, is that you?"

"It sure is. I'm in Charlotte. I just wanted to let you to know that I was back on American soil."

"Oh my God!" I must have cried. To tell the truth, I really can't recall. I must have asked him how long before he'd be home, if there was something special he wanted to eat. It's all a blur now. I do remember feeling engulfed in a mist of joy and my shoulders relaxing as they hadn't in months.

One other thing: I remember going into the bedroom, where I knelt down by the wall and squinched into an inverted V. Then I kicked up. I felt my legs rise oh so easily, until first one, then the other, settled against the wall. I looked out at the room, the ceiling above my feet, the carpet beneath my head. The world was upside down. It was beautiful.

Epilogue

TOURS OF DUTY: A MOTHER'S STORY
(From Commonweal Magazine, 2009)

We were just sitting down to Thanksgiving dinner. Our daughters and their husbands and children chattered nervously, trying to distract me and my husband from thoughts of the one family member who was missing. Our son Mauro had left for Iraq seven months earlier. He was due home soon, but we hadn't heard from him for weeks, and we were nervous. Newspaper stories abounded describing last-minute tragedies—soldiers wounded or killed by Improvised Explosive Devices (IEDs) days before they were scheduled for redeployment. Suddenly, I heard a voice behind me: "Hi, Mom. I'm home."

Mauro had traveled over a hundred hours from Iraq to Washington, D.C., in order to give us the most wonderful Thanksgiving surprise imaginable. The trip had taken him from Ramadi to Kuwait, Germany, South Carolina, and his base in California. From there he had turned around and flown back across the country.

Mauro had wanted to be a Marine since he was a little boy. He had gone to a Jesuit high school and to Georgetown University. He thought that serving in the military would enable him to follow in the Jesuit tradition of being "a man for others."

After 9/11, Mauro was ready to drop everything and rush into battle. He could see the rubble of the Pentagon from the roof of his dorm. Fortunately, the Marines thought he should finish his education first.

When the United States invaded Iraq on March 20, 2003, my son and I supported the action. The Bush administration reported probable connections between Saddam Hussein and Al-Qaida, perpetrators of the 9/11 attacks, and suggested that Saddam had given refuge to other terrorist organizations. Reputable sources like Colin Powell warned that Saddam was producing weapons of mass destruction that could land in the hands of terrorists. Defense Secretary Donald Rumsfeld assured the public that the coming war would be short. "Five days or five weeks or five months, but it certainly isn't going to last any longer than that," he said on Infinity Radio. To be honest, in March 2003, I was anxious for the invasion to start. I wanted to get it over with before Mauro got out of school. On May 24, 2004, the day before his graduation, Mauro was commissioned as a second lieutenant.

The war, of course, was still going on. "How could you let him join the Marines?" friends asked me, as if I hadn't tried to discourage him.

As the president's justifications for going to war started to unravel, I kept my rage to myself. How could I admit that I was conflicted about this enterprise when my son was heading for Iraq? I wanted to be strong and supportive. As one Army mother told me, "You reach a point when you can no longer dwell on the politics of it. All you want is for your kid to come home safe."

After boot camp at Quantico, Mauro left for desert training in California. The young man who was to be his roommate came by the house to help him move. Almar Fitzgerald— they called him "Fitz"—struck me as the consummate officer: intelligent, competent, and courteous. He was a handsome young black man, very solid-looking, with a steady gaze and a soft voice. I remember being proud that my son had chosen such nice friends.

Mauro left for Iraq that summer. He was excited and full of bravado. There was talk of kicking ass and a lot of loud music, the kind that gets young men pumped up. He was to be stationed in Ramadi, in the heart of what Americans have come to call the Sunni Triangle, where he would command a platoon of forty-six men. He called me soon after he arrived. "It's beautiful here," he said. "Full of color! By the way, send cat food, and don't ask questions."

He had adopted two sets of kittens. "Should I send cat litter too?" I asked.

"No, Mom," he laughed. "The whole country is a sandbox!"

But within weeks the banter about kittens ceased. The emails became irregular and cryptic. "You won't hear from me for a few days. I'm busy." He was transferred to another base, but didn't tell me that he was to replace a commander who had been badly wounded. The news in the papers was horrifying. As the casualties mounted, I became addicted to the news, reading three newspapers a day and surfing the Internet for reports on Iraq. Whenever something happened in his area, I'd dash off a frantic message: "Just send word that you're OK." In a few days the answer would come: "I'm OK. Stop reading the papers." Whenever I heard of a Marine dying in another area, I'd feel horror, then relief that it wasn't Mauro, and finally guilt over my relief. Somewhere, I knew, a mother and father were weeping. I kept a backward calendar: 280 days until he's scheduled to come back, 279, 278.... Of course, we didn't have an exact return date, so it was only an estimate.

I rarely slept, and when I did, I had nightmares. I prayed a lot. I became obsessive about calculating survival rates: about a half million have served and 3,000, 3,040, 3,080... have been killed. The chances of Mauro making it back are good, I told myself. But Anbar Province, the stronghold of Sunni resistance to the Shiite-dominated Baghdad government, was a dangerous place, and, anyway, percentages don't matter if it's your kid who's wounded or killed.

Mauro didn't tell me when Fitz died in an IED explosion. I read it in the newspaper. He was just Mauro's age: twenty-three. I cried constantly for four months. I wanted to contact Fitz's mother to offer my condolences, but when I asked my son for the address, he kept putting me off. I knew he had it because when he returned to their shared apartment after completing his tour, he had to gather up his friend's belongings and send them back to Fitz's family. Finally, I stopped asking. I realized that this was his grief, and he wanted to deal with it in his own way. He didn't want me involved. I know it affected him deeply, though. He wore a bracelet with Fitz's name on it for a year.

In Washington, the newspapers ran stories about the Bush girls—what clubs they went to and with whom, what they wore, what they ate. It was a cruel reminder that most of the politicians who were sending our kids to war were making no equivalent sacrifices. Later, when the Bushes were planning Jenna's spectacular wedding, all I could think about were the thousands of military families who had to plan funerals.

After Mauro returned from his first tour, he said very little. It was clear from his clipped responses to my questions that he didn't want to talk. Out of some eight hundred men in his battalion, fourteen died. In a single attack on Mauro's platoon, one Marine was killed and six others lost legs. Mauro went to Walter Reed Hospital to visit those who had been maimed. I found out from newspapers and other sources that he had saved the life of a journalist, pulled two Marines out of a burning vehicle, and dismantled an IED. I'm glad I didn't know about these events while they were happening. Hearing about my son's heroic deeds did not put my mind at ease. I knew he was going back. More disturbing still, he wanted to go back. "You have to fix what you break," he told me. "The only reason for invading a sovereign nation is to leave it in better shape than you found it."

I found him changed. He had lost his bravado. His commitment hadn't faltered: in order to make sense of sacrifices like Fitz's, the country had to forge ahead. But he thought we were going about it in the wrong way. When he talked, which was rarely, it was about the need to confront the root causes of the insurgency and the need for economic development. "It's a war that can't be won solely with weapons," he said. Once back on base in California, Mauro studied Arabic and read extensively on the Middle East and Islam.

One distinctive feature of the Marine Corps' modus operandi is the "debrief," a post-action discussion in which all participants, including junior officers and enlisted men and women, evaluate a recently completed operation. The practice of welcoming input from all members of the unit results not only in increased camaraderie but also in a more efficient fighting force, as good ideas from any source are taken seriously.

Although Mauro met with skepticism at first, he was able to convince his superiors to divide his platoon into units of ten, each of which would be embedded in an Iraqi detachment rather than operating from a U.S. base. By living and working closely with Iraqis, he believed, the Marines would be able to foster a healthier relationship with the people. This might facilitate some new economic development projects that would help to stabilize conflicted areas by giving people a vested interest in keeping things calm. The men formed a plan, and open-minded, supportive superiors helped turn it into reality.

When Mauro returned to Iraq in April 2007, he expected to find Ramadi violent and chaotic, as he had left it. Instead, thanks in part to the "surge" and the Sunni Awakening Councils, the area was relatively quiet. Mauro was assigned to a police station in the Thaylat district, where, as the U.S. commander, he managed a base of ten Marines and between two hundred and three hundred Iraqis.

"The Sunni sheiks had a change of heart," Mauro told me. "They began to realize that they had more to gain by working with us than with Al-Qaida, with its constant diet of intimidation and killing." Of course, the surge entailed certain moral ambiguities: many insurgents cooperated with the Americans because the U.S. military put them on the payroll. Yet it did help to quell the violence in Thaylat and make possible the kinds of projects the platoon hoped to pursue.

At first, the Marines were confronted with widespread distrust. Many inhabitants of Ramadi had lost relatives in the violence. People averted their eyes and walked on when they met U.S. soldiers. The streets were empty and garbage-strewn, and the souk, or marketplace, was moribund.

Mauro began by encouraging his men to build relationships with Iraqis. That meant getting used to new customs. Mauro set the example by eating with Iraqis, seated on the floor and scooping up food with his hands from a common dish. He fasted for Ramadan and broke the fast each night with a different family. He bought livestock to be sent to the mosque to feed the poor. He observed that Iraqi men hug and kiss each other. Sometimes they hold hands, and close friends might even touch each other's thighs during an animated conversation. These gestures contain no sexual innuendo, but they made the Americans uncomfortable. "As guests in their country, we just had to get used to it," Mauro explained.

In order to stimulate economic activity, Mauro directed the men to buy all their supplies in the souk. As they saw Americans circulating freely in the marketplace, local people began to assume that security had improved. Little by little they ventured out to the stalls. By the time the platoon left, its biggest challenges at the marketplace had become traffic and parking.

Mauro tells about a neighborhood tailor who didn't care much for Americans. One day Mauro stopped by his shop and ordered a suit. The tailor made a nice-looking, well-cut garment out of fine English wool. Other Marines started ordering suits, and before long the tailor was showing up regularly at the big American base with bolts of fabric in hand. His attitude toward Americans was changing. "What most Iraqis really want is to work and become self-sufficient," explained Mauro. "By giving this tailor the opportunity to use his skills and sell a product, we helped to restore his sense of self-worth. And we got some nice suits!"

One of Mauro's most frightening stories concerns a barber who refused to deal with the Americans. "I kept going back to his shop and asking for a shave and a haircut, but he always refused," Mauro told me. One day Mauro just sat down in the chair. "Now, you have to realize that Iraqi barbers use a straight razor," Mauro explained, "so I was taking a calculated risk." But it paid off. After that, the attitude of the barber softened and he started cutting the hair of many of the Marines. Mauro is convinced that these small actions produced important changes. "In Iraq, news travels by word of mouth. The tailor and the barber tell their friends that the Americans aren't so bad after all. Every day I saw signs of friendship and bonding."

One day when Mauro was patrolling, he met a man named Yahia, who was a sculptor. During the long and oppressive reign of Saddam Hussein, Yahia had become so distressed that he stopped sculpting and became a carpenter. "He felt that he just couldn't create beautiful objects anymore," Mauro told me. One day Mauro asked Yahia to carve a battalion seal for the commander, Colonel Turner; the men wanted to present it to him as a gift before he left Ramadi. "I gave Yahia a small, post-card-sized picture of our emblem, expecting him to carve a rough likeness into a little piece of wood," laughed Mauro. "I gasped when I saw the finished product. It was a work of art—a gorgeous emblem as large as a tabletop on stained wood." From then on Yahia visited the base daily, and soon he was sculpting again. "He's the best human being I know," said Mauro. "He's pure goodness."

I had no idea what the platoon was doing during this period, as the scarcity of computers on base made emailing almost impossible. I assumed the platoon was still involved in combat. I was amazed when someone sent me a video that showed my son patrolling streets, greeting neighbors in Arabic, hugging men, and laughing with children.

Although he doesn't underestimate the dangers that still beset Iraq, Mauro believes that the vast majority of Iraqis yearn for peace and just want to lead normal lives. He does not see sectarian violence as inevitable. In many communities, he insists, Sunnis and Shiites do live together. When the fiery Shiite cleric Muqtada al-Sadr subjugated areas of Baghdad, many moderate Shiites fled to Ramadi, where Sunnis helped them resettle. "When Iraq won the Asia Cup, we all watched it on TV and cheered!" Mauro told me. "The victory didn't belong to the Sunnis or the Shia. It was an Iraqi victory. The teams were integrated. At that moment, there was a real sense of national unity."

In order to make Thaylat more livable, the Marines cleaned up the streets and initiated reconstruction projects. They fixed sewers and water pipes. Then they began to work with Iraqis to rebuild the area. Schools had been closed because of the violence. Marines and Iraqis refurbished the buildings, replacing broken windows and painting walls. "It was a joy to see little girls sitting in their new classrooms, each one with a colored headscarf, looking up at their teacher," Mauro reported. "We wanted to win over the six-year-olds. Old people are set in their ways, but children grasp new ways. They aren't bound by habit and convention. Slowly, the adults also come to see what a new Iraq can look like. That's why the reconstruction projects were so important."

The Al-Anbar hospital in Ramadi had also been devastated. Equipment was missing or broken, and funds had been squandered. Many doctors had fled to Syria. Patients were routinely turned away without explanation and the remaining doctors worked only from nine to five. The hospital director had no administrative training and constantly threatened to quit. Mauro began paying visits to patients, often late at night, to hear their concerns. He also met with department heads and physicians, encouraging them to communicate with each other. Eventually new rules were established. Patients could no longer be denied services without justification. Doctors accepted shifts so that one of them would always be on duty, day or night. New medicines and equipment were supplied by the Americans.

These activities helped the Americans earn the respect of the local inhabitants and created a sense of security. Little by little, signs of hope appeared. People started restoring their houses. "They never did that during our first tour," Mauro noted, "because bombs were going off all the time." As the Marines earned their trust, Ramadi's citizens began reporting suspicious activity and weapons caches to them.

Mauro saw the exclusion of women from the political and economic life of the city as a moral issue as well as a security risk. The role of women was a delicate matter, however, because Mauro wanted to show sensitivity toward Islamic customs. As base commander, he ran the city council meetings and suggested a woman be present at all of them. Once he got to know the town elders fairly well, they were willing to comply. "The women brought a special perspective," Mauro explained. Now that the area was stable, they wanted to be able to go out with their children. The Marines responded by building a park with the help of donations from the people of Thaylat. The women also wanted public transportation, since they do not drive and taxis are expensive. So Mauro's team helped put in a bus system.

Mauro credited two "sharp, tough civilians" with facilitating this work. Donna Carter, of the Department of Defense, worked with the women. John Gerlaugh, a counterterrorism expert and retired Marine, connected the platoon with influential people at the State Department. Both were members of the Provincial Reconstruction Team. One impressive project was a women's union that facilitated microloans to help establish businesses. The women themselves started a daycare system and even a gym. "The change in them was visible," said Mauro. "When I first arrived in Iraq, they were all wearing black burqas. By the time I left, they were still wearing burqas, but in colors—pink, green, turquoise. That shows a change in attitude." The Iraqis indicated their appreciation by naming him an honorary sheik.

Looking back, Mauro is quick to point out

that his experience in Iraq was limited to two seven-month tours in one small corner of the country. He is wary of making generalizations or predictions about the future. Not only is it not his place to do so, but it is too early to know whether the progress made in areas like Thaylat will have a lasting effect. This is not a war between nations that will end with surrender and a treaty.

Certainly, challenges remain. The spike in violence in April, 2009, when 371 Iraqis and 18 Americans were killed, is cause for grave concern. Attacks in Sadr City and the deaths of 80 Iranian pilgrims on their way to the Imam Musa al-Kadhim shrine, one of the holiest in Shiite Islam, could exacerbate sectarian conflict. On May 4, a U.S.-backed militia leader was arrested and charged with terrorism, showing that not all our Sunni allies are reliable. At Camp Ashraf, which holds more than three thousand members of the Iranian opposition group PMOI, Iraqi authorities are reportedly withholding fuel and medicine from the inhabitants, including women and children, despite protests from the European Parliament and Amnesty International. And tensions still exist between Arabs and Kurds in Kurdistan. President Barack Obama has stressed that extreme caution is required as U.S. troops prepare to leave Iraq by the end of 2011, so that the progress we have made is not undone. Hardly a day goes by when there isn't another article in a major newspaper about the "fragile and reversible" situation in Iraq.

As an American, I can only hope for the best. As a mother, I see Mauro's second tour as a spiritually transformative experience for him. By working with Iraqi civilians, he was able to appreciate the humanity of people he had previously seen as enemies. He developed as a man for others by being able to see others as men... and women. Mauro's story is that of many young people who find themselves profoundly altered by their experiences in war zones. Of course, Mauro was lucky. Contributing to the reconstruction of Thaylat gave him a true sense of accomplishment and, to a degree, helped to vindicate the sacrifice of cherished friends like Fitz. For many others who served multiple tours, the second and third were as bad as the first, making the healing process much more difficult. And, of course, nearly 4,300 soldiers never made it back.

Although Mauro answered my questions for this article, he remains reticent about his experience in Iraq. He wants to move forward, not dwell in the past. I realize that many readers of this magazine considered the war to be wrong and immoral from the very start. Nevertheless, I think it is important to know about some of the constructive things our men and women in uniform are accomplishing. Most people know little about the day-to-day lives of our soldiers or the relationships many have forged with individual Iraqis. These stories deserve to be told. No matter what our opinions on the war, we can appreciate the extraordinary achievements of our men and women in uniform.

I expected Mauro to look for a job in defense or government when he left the Marines, but he refused to consider those avenues. Instead, he applied to graduate schools and was accepted by the Kellogg School of Management. "I have seen war," he says. "I want to devote the rest of my life to peace." He believes economic development and the integration of women will create more just, stable societies; and he is anxious to bring the lessons he learned in Ramadi to other post-conflict areas.

About the Author

Bárbara Mujica is a novelist, short-story writer, essayist, and scholar. Her international bestseller *Frida* has appeared in 18 languages and was a Book-of-the-Month alternate. *Sister Teresa* was adapted for the stage by The Actor's Studio in Hollywood. *I Am Venus* was a Maryland Writers Association National Fiction Competition winner in the category Historical Fiction and a quarter-finalist in the 2020 ScreenCraft Cinematic Novel Competition. Mujica's collection of stories, *Far from My Mother's Home* (Spanish edition: *Lejos de la casa de mi madre*) focuses on the immigrant experience.

Mujica has won several prizes for her writing, including the E.L. Doctorow International Fiction Competition, the Pangolin Prize, and the Theodore Christian Hoepfner Award for short fiction. Three of the stories included in *Imagining Iraq* have been winners of the Maryland Writers' Association National Fiction Competition in the category Short Story: "Imagining Iraq" (third prize, 2010), "Jason's Cap" (first prize, 2015), "Ox" (second prize, 2016).

Mujica's scholarly books include *Religious Women and Epistolary Culture in the Carmelite*

Reform: The Disciples of Teresa de Ávila; Teresa de Ávila, Lettered Woman; and *Teresa de Jesús: Espiritualidad y feminismo*; as well as the edited volumes *Women Writers of Early Modern Spain: Sophia's Daughters* and *A New Anthology of Early Modern Spanish Theater: Play and Playtext.*

Mujica is a professor emerita at Georgetown University, where she taught Spanish literature. The mother of a Marine, she was Faculty Adviser of the GU Student Veterans Association and co-chair of the Veterans Support Team, a coalition of administrators, faculty, and students striving to make Georgetown a more veteran-friendly campus. She was awarded the University President's Medal for her work on behalf of veterans in 2015.

Her book *Collateral Damage*, an edited collection of women's war-writing, originated in a symposium she organized at Georgetown called "Women Who Write about War."

www.barbaramujica.com

Acknowledgments

These stories originally appeared in the following publications:

"Imagining Iraq," in *O-Dark-Thirty*.

"Ahmed the Tailor," in *Stories though the Ages: Baby Boomers Plus 2020*.

"Jason's Cap," in *Synergy: A Collage of Voices [Anthology]*.

"The Chaplain," in *Consequence Magazine*.

"Green Eyes," in *Forge Journal*.

"Judgment," in *The Report*.

"Who the Hell Is Rosie Méndez?," in *Trivia: Voices of Feminism*.

"The Last Mission," in *DAP (The Diverse Arts Project)*.

"Interrogating Calla," in *Halfway down the Stairs*.

"The Call," in *Serving House Journal of the Literary Arts*.

"A Lucky Son of a Bitch," in *The Blue Lake Review*.

"A Good Old American Breakfast," in *The Report*.

"Ox," in *Letras femeninas*.

"Captain O'Reilly and the Professor," in *Tayo Literary Magazine*.

"Prejudice," in *Stories through the Ages: Baby Boomers Plus 2017.*

"Upside Down," in *Reed Magazine.*

"Tours of Duty: A Mother's Story," in *Commonweal Magazine*

CPSIA information can be obtained
at www.ICGtesting.com
Printed in the USA
FSHW020721090921
84515FS